The Belle

The Belle of Nauvoo

A Novel of Love and Betrayal

Becky Paget

(author of *Romancing the Nephites*)

Covenant Communications Inc.

Cover illustration by Daniel Johnson

Published by Covenant Communications, Inc.
American Fork, Utah

Printed in the United States of America
First Printing: April 1994

94 95 96 97 98 99 00   10 9 8 7 6 5 4 3 2

ISBN 1-55503-690-2

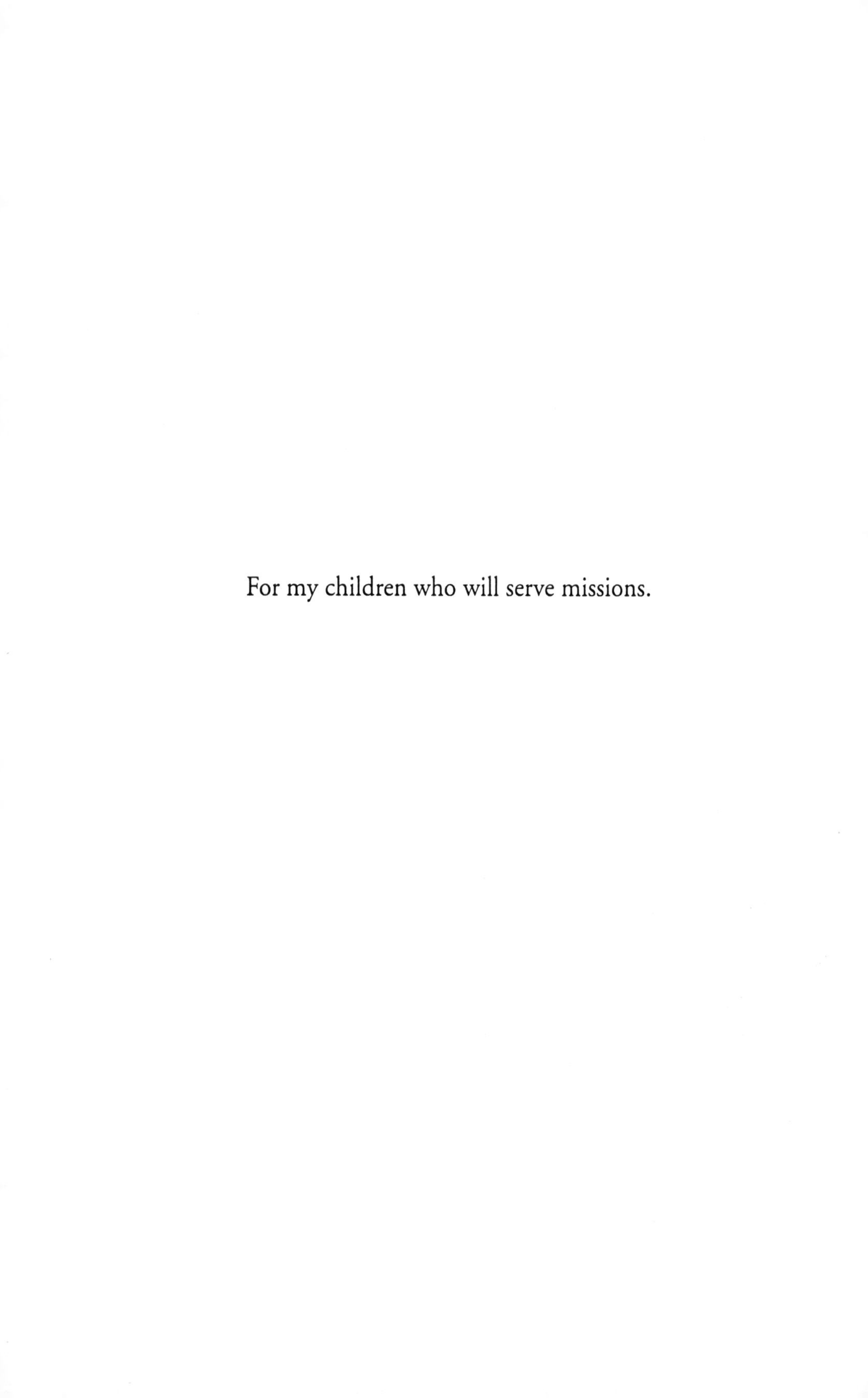

For my children who will serve missions.

Acknowledgments

Many people were of tremendous help to me as I prepared this manuscript under a tight deadline. I started with Christy Petersen, who told me about Emma Smith. My friends, Debbie and Michael Boucha, had a free evening to spend at the Family History Center in Salt Lake City. I met Paul Hokensen, who lives in St. Louis and is the Historical Committee Chairman of the Smith Family Organization. Without him, I could not have written this novel. He loaned me countless books and theses, answered the most obscure questions I had, and even did some editing for me.

Two brothers in the Walker family, Kay and Gene, shared their genealogy with me. Friends loaned me books: Sharon Fortner, the Greene family, and the Hardins. I drove to Southern Illinois University at Edwardsville and unlocked the Mormon file, a rarely-used and rich source of information put together by Stanley Kimball. Also very helpful were the Church historical librarians, the BYU librarians, and the Nauvoo Restoration missionaries who put up with me for two days. An unknown RLDS employee gave me a tour of the Mansion House, and I thank him.

People who were able to answer my many questions included Mike Trapp of Nauvoo, Elder Backman of Nauvoo Restoration, Susan Easton Black, Michael Moody of the Church Music Committee, Bishop Egon Wetzker, and Gregg Edwards with his new Infobase program.

I could never adequately thank my friends who helped me edit—Barbara Lewis and Suellen Johnson. They were there just when I needed them. I thank my friends who encouraged me, especially Susan Temple. And I am especially grateful to the youth of the South St. Louis Stake for helping me believe in this project by listening to me talk about it for one full hour without getting too bored. That was my greatest miracle. I also thank my family for their support. But most of all, I thank my Heavenly Father for his help, because he poured out more blessings upon me than I deserve.

Chapter One

I had just settled down for the night and fallen asleep under my quilts, when I was awakened by what I believed to be a choir of angels singing in the birth of the Christ child. It was Christmas in Nauvoo, 1843. I was sixteen—the most wonderful of all ages, when life was full of countless possibilities and marriage lay just around the corner.

I heard my younger brothers running to their windows, throwing them open and hailing the angelic choirs. I too rushed to my window and threw up the sash, finding an earthly choir firmly standing upon the ground creating the angelic sounds. It was glorious! They sang:

Mortals, awake! with angels join,
And chant the solemn lay;
Love, joy, and gratitude combine
To hail the auspicious day.
In heav'n the rapt'rous song began,
And sweet seraphic fire
Through all the shining legions ran,
And swept the sounding lyre.

I waved to my acquaintances among the young men and women in the group. Can you wonder that I believed it to be a choir of angels? Sister Lettice Rushton, the blind sister from England, and her family, friends, and neighbors performed the kind service of serenading our family and that of the Prophet Joseph Smith, my uncle. Both he and my father, Hyrum Smith, still dressed, went out into the street to listen to the carollers and speak with them. The Law family and other neighbors, and the boarders at the Mansion House who were still awake, joined them outdoors.

Down through the portals of the sky
The pealing anthem ran,
And angels flew, with eager joys
To bear the news to man.

As Father was still awake and busy at that late hour, I wondered what on earth St. Nicholas was placing at my breakfast plate—perhaps a new hat pin or lace collar! I dearly wanted a lace collar for my newly-made dress to wear to the party on Christmas Day. As the song they sang was seven verses long, I had ample time to wonder greatly. But 'twas one of my favorites and rendered with pure and simple voices:

Hail, Prince of Life, forever hail!
Redeemer, brother, friend!
Though earth, and time, and life should fail,
Thy praise shall never end.

At the song's conclusion, both carollers and neighbors were friendly and full of the spirit of Christmas. My brother John shouted several greetings out the window to our cousin Joseph, his firm friend, both boys being age eleven. Others of the Prophet's household also appeared at the windows, and I waved to my bosom companions Eliza and Emily Partridge, the Lawrence girls, and Lucy Walker. However, when her brother Lorin Walker leaned out of a window, I withdrew my own head quickly. I was wrapped in a tattered wool shawl, and I could never let Lorin Walker see me looking that way!

However, that brief glimpse of my favorite beau set my heart beating in my breast in anticipation of his favors the next day during the party. We would both dine and dance. Would he entreat me to dance a waltz? Would he ask me to dance more than one time? Whom else would he bestow his favors upon? Lorin was a very popular young man, a good man who gave most of his time to the building of the temple. He also kept the arms for the whole Nauvoo Legion and the receipts for the Young Gentlemen's and Ladies' Relief Society. He showed tremendous promise and had the confidence of his temporary father, my uncle Joseph. (His family had become part of my uncle's when his father was sent on a mission and his mother died.) So naturally, several of the girls who were eligible for marriage sought his favor, though none more than I. And I had the privilege of intimacy with my uncle's family, which gave me a decided advantage in the chase.

"Lovina! John! Shut the windows tight and climb back into your beds. Breakfast comes early!" Mother called from downstairs. She was my stepmother, but very dear to me. When my own mother had died, Father had courted and wed Mary Fielding, a convert from England. How she labored, through her teachings and kindnesses, to provide Father's poor orphaned children with a loving mother. And how she succeeded! I loved her as if she were my own flesh and blood.

Obediently, though cautiously, lest I be sighted in my unbecoming attire by a certain young gentleman, I put down the sash and crawled between my icy sheets. My bedroom was freezing! Finding the wrapped warm bricks in my bed and placing one at my feet and one against the small of my back, I settled down to the sweet anticipation of a marriageable girl's favorite pastime—dancing on Christmas Day.

Chapter Two

"Ought we to let her attend?" Mother asked her husband Hyrum. "Joseph came expressly to warn us of the questionable characters who put their names down to attend the dinner."

"Papa! You must let me go to the dinner! You must!" I turned the most sorrowful eyes that I could summon to my countenance upon that one parent, my father, with full knowledge of the effect such a look had worked upon him in times past.

Papa stared into my eyes and wavered.

Mother added, "A girl must have a care for her reputation. A good name endureth forever."

"Oh, Papa! Please!!" I beseeched him.

"How can I deny her?"

Ah! I was about to prevail. Aunt Mercy Thompson, who was Mother's widowed sister, lived in our home at the time. She intervened to the satisfaction of all parties. "Perhaps you might chaperon her, Hyrum. We can sacrifice your company for such a cause as this, and no one will dare give insult to Lovina with her own father in attendance."

I smiled on Aunt Mercy. Bless her.

Father smiled. "Where is this glorious creation you ladies have been sewing upon for so many weeks? Put it on! I'm anxious to see what kind of girl I'll be escorting today!"

"Do you think your knee can stand the strain, Hyrum?" asked

Mother Mary.

Once again I held my breath. Father had injured his knee earlier in the month and had been largely confined to the house.

"I think it might hold up under the circumstances. Sound as a wood beam, it is."

I threw my arms around my father and kissed him soundly. "Thank you, Papa. You won't be sorry! I'll be ready in two shakes of a cat's tail," I said, then rushed to the stairs and climbed them. However, my preparations took anything but a moment, for I meant to be seen at my best that afternoon. My crinoline petticoats were scented with lavender and my hair was curled in English ringlets with the hot tongs.

Ever so gently, Aunty Grinnels, our housekeeper, and Mother lowered the dress over my tresses and laced the back buttons. I looked at it one part at a time in my mirror, and thought myself fit to come before the throne of God. If not that, at least fit to turn the heads of a few young men! My dress was a frothy creation of tucks and laces—all pink. We placed the English point lace I had found on my plate that morning around my corsage to form a collar. The lace had travelled all the way from Preston, England. I felt rich as the queen herself. We both had dark hair and were small. The color of my dress gave my skin a glow that needed no dusting of cochineal powder. With that and a sparkle in my eye, I was fair set to dazzle all my beaus.

The whole family gathered at the foot of the stairs for my descent. The younger girls, Jerusha and Mary Jane, Sarah, and baby Martha Ann, were awestruck by my transformation. Even my brothers, John and little Joseph F., had to appreciate the triumph of the collective labors of four women. I was ready for the dance.

Father lifted his arm with pride, and I placed my gloved hand upon his elbow. His other hand held his cane to favor his knee. We left the house.

As the family watched us cross the street, a face at each windowpane, Father confided to me how much I was like my mother,

Jerusha, when she was sixteen.

"I courted her for years before I had a home to bring her to. She was worth waiting for." He stopped and turned to look at me. "You bring those days in Palmyra back to me. I am as proud of you as I was of her."

I felt my bosom swell at his praise so lavishly given. "Th- thank you, Papa. I only hope I can be worthy of my mother and meet her again."

"I, too, hope for such a moment."

Perhaps I was a bit too grateful for my new dress and my father's praises; but when I recollect the troublous scenes through which I had passed in my earlier years, bereft of home, father, adequate food, and at times even shoes in the winter, my thoughts that day might be forgiven.

We entered the door of the Mansion House. It was the home and hotel of my Uncle Joseph and Aunt Emma Smith. Aunt Emma ran the business, and Uncle Joseph ran the Church. Never did a family deserve a fine home more than they, for they had passed through the same trying scenes as we had with the rest of the Saints. For years they had boarded with others until they finally had a home of their own, which was the one in which we were now living. A month previous we had moved into the Old Homestead at Water and Main while our new and larger home was being built. With church business and visitors, our tiny home had become much too cramped. I loved living so close to my friends in the Mansion.

The Mansion was a fitting reward for Uncle Joseph's and Aunt Emma's sacrifices, and it was a presage to the mansions they would inherit above. As they had for so many years shared their bread and board with all and sundry in need or want, they were now able to do so on a much larger scale. Some people thought Uncle Joseph was rich because he lived in a grand new house, but I knew better. I had often seen him give away his last coin to the poor.

The front hall of the Mansion was festooned with strings of fir tied with bunches of waxed crabapples. On the table, nestled in a bed of pine needles, sat a scene of the holy family cut from paper. Above it a candle burned in representation of the Star of Bethlehem. Such a sight heightened my anticipation of beauteous glories that might decorate the party.

"Brother Hyrum! What brings you here today?" said Dr. Bernheisel, a resident of the Mansion.

"Just came to see that Lovina comes to no harm from the gossipmongers today.

"Ah. Several of the girls are remaining at home, much to the disappointment of the young gentlemen!"

My friends who lived in the Mansion came into the hall and exclaimed over my dress. "Lovina! What a delicious dress!"

"You nigh overpower me!"

"Was the lace collar your Christmas gift? Lucky, lucky girl!"

I was swallowed up in their circle and carried away to the kitchens. They were the largest kitchens I had ever seen, large enough to cook a meal for several hundred people. The fireplace covered one whole end of the wall. Six pots could boil at once. The kitchen also had two of those new iron stoves. Today the cooks were bustling about in preparation for two large dinners. There was to be a party for the adults after ours.

Lucy Walker told me, "Eliza and Emily have permission from Sister Emma to attend the dinner with us if we serve for tonight's party." They both had on their party dresses, but neither was new like mine. And neither had a collar of English point lace.

"How splendid that will be!" I was most anxious for their company. It was kind of Aunt Emma to allow them this treat in view of the amount of work the day entailed. Upon the death of their father, Bishop Edward Partridge, Eliza and Emily had come to work for Aunt Emma and had stayed to help with the Mansion House when it opened last summer. I had become intimately acquainted with them.

Aunt Emma had taken in others, too—the Lawrence orphans and the whole Walker family. Lucy and Catherine Walker were also my friends, though I was much closer to Lucy. The Walkers were all my "adopted" cousins. We loved one another very much and could not be separated.

Emily said, "Lucy's coming too. She arranged with Olive to do her work early." Olive had recently married William Walker, the oldest of the Walker children. They helped run the Mansion House.

"Have you seen the guest list?" asked Eliza Partridge.

"Not yet," I answered.

She whispered, "There are those on the list who are believed to be blacklegs and slickers and others of questionable character." Mother had been right. "No! However did that happen?"

Her sister Emily whispered, "Sister Emma allowed it."

Lucy explained, "She's very anxious to make a success of the Mansion House enterprise and wanted a full table."

"Oh, my!" I exclaimed. "Whatever shall we do? It will be the end of our reputations if we dance with one of them. We will have to be most circumspect."

"That isn't all," said Emily. "Sylvester Emmonds came over and hung a kissing ball! We are in a most precarious position."

"A kissing ball! No wonder Mother didn't encourage my attendance!" Sylvester Emmonds was a gentile visitor, though an acceptable young man in society. The evening might indeed prove too much for my innocence—but not once did it cross my mind to retreat from it.

Emily added, "Brother Joseph allowed the kissing ball only if the young men constrain themselves to kissing the backs of hands."

Eliza whispered, "Helen Kimball's father put his foot down and she can't come, but Horace fooled him and is coming. However did you talk Brother Hyrum into allowing you here?"

"Father came with me."

"On Christmas Day?" Emily asked.

I picked up a spoon to stir the applesauce and said, "Aunt Mercy suggested that they might sacrifice him. I'm afraid it would have been a far greater sacrifice to hang my new dress in the closet after they worked so hard to sew it!"

"Well, if you will be helping us in the kitchen," said Lucy, "you had better cover that divine dress with a large apron or it will be a sacrifice for naught."

Eliza added, "And if you stand so close to the fire, you are bound to singe your hem. That would be a crime."

Aunt Emma Smith overheard that and said, "Nonsense, girls. Lovina is to do no work today. All of you go and join the party. Olive has things under control and is ready to serve."

Giving my aunt a rapturous greeting, I said, "Aunt Emma, Merry Christmas! Thank you so much for the perfect party! It's the best in all the world! How do you like my new dress?"

"Merry Christmas, Lovina, my favorite niece." She held me back from her. "That dress is enough to set the angels singing. I believe Brother Hyrum does spoil you, but you look a fair vision."

"Oh, do you really think I do?"

"Yes. And I think a certain young man will, too."

My eyes grew large and I looked around to see if anyone had overheard her. "Who?" I dared to inquire.

Aunt Emma gave me a knowing smile and whispered, "Lorin."

Chapter Three

As the poet says, the eloquent blood spoke in my cheeks. I had need to hide those cheeks behind my fan when I saw the object of my desires milling about with the gentlemen. Every time I saw Lorin Walker this happened to me. As it never occurred in the presence of other young men, I took it as a sign that he was the beau meant for me. Several of my favorites were with him—Garrett Ivins, James Monroe, Horace Whitney, and William Cutler. But Lorin Walker was my most favorite beau. He was the first of the Walker children to stay with Uncle Joseph; and from the time I first met him standing in Uncle Joseph's yard by the well, I adored him, though I was much too young to be noticed by such an older boy. (He was five years my senior.) I was shy of him then, also. He ran errands for Uncle Joseph and often came to our home on Water Street. When he came, I would grow quiet and ladylike, hoping he would notice me.

Lorin grew up to have a noble bearing, yet he kept his merry heart and great love for the Lord. We became acquainted. During the past year, when we had served together in the Young Gentlemen's and Ladies Relief Society in assisting the poor, he had proved both resourceful and dependable. His brow was wide and clear and intelligent. Though he did not wear clothes that were distinguished by refinement, his cravats were tied with a dash that I could not help but admire. And he owned a great tall chestnut horse that was almost as fine as Old Charley, my uncle's horse.

Eliza, Emily, and Lucy were already in the dining room when I came from speaking with my aunt. They were trading the names set at the different places on the tables, and I asked them, "Whatever can you be about, switching the place cards?"

"Don't worry Lovina, you will be in amiable company," Eliza explained. "We are making certain that we are, also."

"Oh. With whom am I to dine?"

"Sister Emma placed you beside Lorin. Would you like your card to stay there?" asked his sister, Lucy.

Would I like it to stay there? Had ever a more nonsensical question been asked? "Yes, that will be fine," I answered demurely, clutching my bag tightly at the thought. I was still too shy about my tender feelings for Lorin to share them. Other young men I might boast about, but not Lorin.

My friends giggled. I suspected that they were aware of my sentiments.

I let my eyes wander about the dining room to behold its magnificence. One hundred places were set with china, and a dais was placed at the end of the dining hall for the orchestra. All about the room hung boughs of holly and ivy with red paper ribbons. In the center of each table stood molded candy animals and stretched candy towers, all red. The rest of the tables were adorned with pine boughs, hard springerly cookies, seed pods, and corn-husk angels. At each windowpane hung a star made from welded nails that would later be broken apart to use for the temple. Two corners of the room held Christmas trees covered with popcorn strings, tatted lace snowflakes, cookie cutters, wax-dipped cookies, and candles. There were also candles on the chandeliers, which were not lighted because it was still daylight. The scene was glorious beyond words.

Dinner was every bit as delectable as the decor. Roast pheasant was served with stuffing, applesauce, and roasted potatoes. Dessert was catered by the newly-opened Scovil's bakery. All of this was remarked upon at great length.

In consequence of the amiable conversation I engaged in with

Lorin, and perhaps because of the way I looked in my new lace collar, he asked me for the first dance, a French four.

The general and his lady opened the dance. Uncle Joseph was dressed in his bright blue uniform with shiny brass buttons glittering down its front. Aunt Emma was in gray muslin du lain. They made a handsome pair.

As Lorin and I began our dance, my eyes sparkled and my cheeks were rosy, not entirely due to exertion. I'm afraid my companions imagined quite a romance in the air between Lorin and myself. Lucy could not resist teasing me as we passed in the movements of the dance. "Methinks me brother is fair smitten with thee," she quipped.

"Hush, Lucy, whatever will he think?" I implored her.

But Lucy would not stop, and whispered the next time we passed, "The girls are set to tear you apart with jealousy, Lovina Smith." My eyes wandered to Sarah Rigdon standing under the kissing ball with Joseph Jackson, a young man and a gentile, who was said to have been a Catholic priest. Mr. Jackson took Sarah by her hand, turned it over, and placed two lingering kisses right on her wrist- as they do in Italy! So much for Mr. Jackson's vows! The Rigdon girls were not permitted to dance, so when they had parties they played games instead. I had heard that the Rigdons' games were kissing games, and now I believed it.

My eyes caught those of my partner, and his twinkled with merriment. He had witnessed the kiss also. "Now, don't you think those things, Lorin Walker," I told him. "We will dance firmly on this side of the room."

"With you I will . . ." he teased.

"Lorin Walker, you wouldn't dare! Why, you are treasurer of the Young Gentlemen's and Ladies Relief Society! That would be against all the society's principles. You must set the example!"

"I might let your dare remain unchallenged if you promise me two more dances," he said before we were separated by the dance movements.

Two more dances! Why, that was practically a declaration of

his intentions! My heart thrilled at this evidence of his desire for my company! When we came back together and he took my fingers and bowed to me I responded, "I shall be happy to champion your virtue, but you'll have to ask the permission of two other gentlemen."

"And who might they be?"

I am sorry to say that I was at moments overcome by all the attention I was receiving from the young men since my coming of age. However, I was sensible enough to realize, with the aid of timely reminders from my stepmother, that this was due to my being the niece of the general and daughter of the church patriarch more than my own consequence. A few gentlemen had even sought their salvation by an attempt to marry into the Smith clan via myself. Father called it shirt-tail salvation and had sent them packing. I needed to be a careful judge of character and was often aided in this by my family—grandmother, aunts, and uncles. They each one sought to row an oar in my romances.

I smiled at Lorin and replied, "There are so many that I am afraid I can't remember them all. Is there one here you might name who owes you a kindness?"

"A kindness? They would have to be quite in my debt to persuade them away from so lovely and popular a young lady as yourself."

"Now you flatter me!" I laughed, suspecting that Lorin was teasing me for my beaus. I looked at my dance card and saw one partner who might be persuaded. "How about William Kimball?" I suggested. "He'll do anything for someone who won't tell his father that he could have got his money back for the party when Brother Kimball refused to allow him to attend. He's engaged me for the third dance."

"The deed is done. And the sixth dance? It's a waltz," he added significantly. One came in close contact with one's partner when dancing a waltz.

"I'm afraid that is promised to Joseph Jackson."

Lorin got a mulish look on his face when I told him that.

"Then you are dancing the sixth dance with me! I'm not letting him dance you under that kissing ball."

"Yes, Lorin," I agreed meekly. And who says that a woman does not enjoy obeying her man? That was the most pleasurable agreement that I ever made. Three dances in one evening! The gossips would really have something to chew on after that.

William Kimball was so anxious to oblige Lorin by resigning his dances that several other young men also took advantage of his circumstances. I'm afraid he didn't have a very good time at the party after all. He left with some dissatisfaction in his breast and a lesson learned that it is not wise to deceive one's parent. At the conclusion of William's forfeited set of dances, I had such a hope that perhaps my regard for Lorin was returned by him to the exact same degree, that I thought it no great evil to put off Joseph Jackson for the sixth set.

To my dismay, Mr. Jackson was not nearly so amiable about the switch in partners as was William Kimball, and he would not give me up.

Lorin arrived at my side with a pleasurable smile on his face. "Is all arranged between us?" he asked.

I knew not what to say. I desperately wished to dance that third dance with Lorin, but did not know how to appease Mr.Jackson.

"The dance was promised to me," Mr. Jackson reiterated.

"Our hostess suggested a trade of partners. You are privileged to partner Eliza Partridge," Lorin informed him.

I hid my face behind my fan. Clever Lorin, to get Aunt Emma to help.

Joseph Jackson clicked his heels with obvious displeasure and went to talk to Aunt Emma, who directed his attention to Eliza, sitting with Emily. Eliza looked none too pleased when he looked in her direction. What had I done? Was I giving displeasure to my friend? My concern for Eliza nearly spoiled my borrowed dance.

My conscience was partially eased when I gazed in the direction of my father and Uncle Joseph and read the obvious approval on their faces when they noticed that I was dancing with Lorin for the third time. Those family matchmakers! Also anxious to further my cause with Lorin, Aunt Emma graciously took the elbows of both Joseph Jackson and Sylvester Emmonds and led them to my two friends for partners. She must have said something, for Mr. Jackson suddenly appeared very much recovered from his disappointment. Eliza and Emily also appeared to be reconciled to the trade, which relieved my conscience considerably. I gave myself up to the exquisite pleasure of waltzing with Lorin. I only hoped my friends could stay clear of the kissing ball!

Chapter Four

The day after Christmas was English Boxing Day, and with so many English converts celebrating it, we did also. My mother's kitchen was filled with young men enjoying my company after their chores were done. I was still baking the bread, and according to Mother and Aunt Mercy, the young men were eating it faster than I could bake it.

I held up a bowl of maple sugar drops and they all begged for a taste. "Just one, please," begged Andrew Cahoon.

I popped one right into his mouth, and then of course had to do the same thing for all the others. They were Garrett Ivins, William Cutler, and Marcellus Bates. Mother's mouth set in a straight line as she watched me, and I blushed as I realized I was behaving in a forward manner. I was not shy with these young men, for they were like brothers to me. To cover up my impropriety, I put one drop each into my sisters' mouths also. At times it was hard not to get too carried away with my own consequence. "Lovina, remember you promised to collect for the fund today," Mother reminded me. Father had started the sisters contributing a penny per week to save up for glass and nails for the temple. It was called the Penny Fund. Everyone who subscribed had their name recorded in the Book of the Law of the Lord.

I was putting a candy into my own mouth, but stopped abruptly and said, "Oh, dear! I nearly forgot. This bread is taking such an extraordinary time to bake that I'm afraid I'll not have time to collect."

"I'm sure it can be arranged," Mother said with a touch of sarcasm.

"I'll take you!" Garrett Ivins eagerly offered. He jumped from his seat. "My carriage is just down the street."

"Mine is outside," Andrew Cahoon countered with a bow. Then all the others offered their services also. How was I to choose? Four young men wanted my company. Oh, my! It was a most gratifying situation. They were lined up before me. Should I choose one or two, or would it be better to allow them all to accompany me at once? Or would that cause gossip? I knew not which one of my beaus to choose.

I was saved by a knock on the kitchen door and the entry of Lorin. Here was my clear choice! Immediately perceiving the advantages of this timely interruption to my quandary, I crossed the room to him. My heart was thumping like a hammer at the sight of him, and I was afraid that all of them could tell that my smile was grander for Lorin than for them. I was not as yet ready to relinquish so much admiration from all my beaus, yet I could not help favoring Lorin.

"Just the man to solve our difficulty!" exclaimed Marcellus Bates, welcoming Lorin to their circle. "Lovina must go collecting and needs to choose an escort. Each one of us has offered to accompany her. Now you must be an impartial judge and choose her escort."

"Is that agreed?" Lorin asked all my beaus.

"Agreed," they said in unison.

Lorin put his hand on his chin, as if thinking deeply, "Hmmm . . . and you promise to abide by my judgment with no hurt feelings?"

"Agreed," they repeated earnestly.

"Then, as an impartial judge, I choose myself," he said with a huge smile.

There were cries of "Not fair!" and "You are taking advantage!" But to my secret delight, Lorin's claim prevailed. I thought him most clever.

Mother and Aunt Mercy laughed.

"Porter Rockwell is back from the Missouri jail. He's over at the Mansion right now," Lorin told us as he sat down.

"'Twas quite an event last night," Mother remarked.

Several of the boys expressed a wish that they had been witness to Porter Rockwell's arrival.

"Were you there when he came in?" I asked Lorin.

"Sure thing. I was one of those who held his arm ready to put him out the door when we all thought he was a drunk Missourian. Porter came in all dirty, with his hair long and unkempt from being in prison so long. He'd lost a good thirty pounds and was staggering around, putting on an act to fool us. No one knew him at all. Then Brother Joseph grabbed him by the arms to get a good look in his enemy's face—you know how Brother Joseph does. To our surprise, he then drew his enemy to his breast and wept. We all thought that was carrying forgiveness a few steps too far until he held him back again and cried, 'Porter Rockwell!' What a celebration they had after that! It'll go down in the annals of the Lord."

"It must have been so thrilling!" I cried. My eyes were shining with love and admiration for Lorin, not Porter Rockwell.

My beaus looked from me to Lorin and back again, then one by one paid their respects to Mother and Aunt Mercy and left. After that I never again had so many beaus to call on me at once. Lorin had won my heart and they all knew it.

Thus Lorin and I began a much steadier courtship with that walk through Nauvoo to collect pennies. I put on my warmest cloak and thickest wool petticoat to protect me from the bitter wind and we went out into the cloudy day. However, there was sunshine in my heart, yea, even springtime, and I felt little of the cold. Had I had gone with Garrett Ivins or Andrew Cahoon, I could have driven and accomplished my task in a quarter of the time. But I had no desire to speed my journey, and neither did Lorin.

We stopped at the homes of Sisters Law, Marks, and Johnson, then on to Sisters Wright, Miller, and Williams. After that we collected down Sidney Street at the Shearers', Eldredges', Stewarts' and Allreds'. That covered my whole route for the day. My pouch was full.

"Sister Emma contributed two chickens for the price of two tickets to the concert tomorrow night. Would you care to accompany me?" Lorin asked.

My breast filled with dismay as I realized I had already committed to accompany Horace Whitney. I knew not how to reply, for I wanted to go with Lorin with every particle of my heart; yet could not release myself from my promise. Members of the Whitney family were among our oldest and dearest friends; they had sheltered us and housed the Smiths in my early youth. And I did admire Horace. He did not deserve such shabby treatment.

"What did you say, Lovina?"

I said nothing and rubbed my mittens together nervously.

"I know it is rather late to ask . . ."

I stopped and turned to Lorin with agony in my eyes. Placing my glove to my lips, I said, "It is too late. I already promised Horace Whitney. It is a promise I dare not break."

Lorin smiled anyway. "It's enough to know you would rather go with me."

"Oh, I would! I would!" I assured him with great earnestness.

"That's good enough," he said cheerfully and began to whistle. "I will take Lucy or Catherine with me and gaze upon your beauty from afar."

"You're teasing me now," I protested.

He stopped his whistling and turned to me. "I'm not, you know. To me you are the most beautiful girl in Nauvoo." He quoted: "Softly she treads upon the daisies, lest she dim their glory by her own."

I was inordinately pleased by his compliment and knew not where to look. Once again my blushes overcame me. Perhaps I could easily do without the admiration of my other beaus! But all

I said was, "Surely you have seen prettier girls in St. Louis."

Lorin bowed. "No, madam. I amend that compliment to 'the prettiest girl in all the great wide world.'"

"That is most gratifying," I whispered, thinking to myself that they were not just gratifying words—they were fit to make the seraphim sing! Lorin favored me above all others!

He put his arm out for my hand. I felt this to be symbolic of our new relationship. Shyly I tucked my glove into the warm crook of his coat, and we continued our stroll down the frozen road. I left my hand there for the remainder of the journey. The pink sunset glowed over the silvery blue expanse of the frozen Mississippi River. It was like a journey towards heaven.

Chapter Five

Between then and the New Year, Lorin was in our home every day, often bringing more news to us from the Mansion House and the outside world than our own father. By Saturday night, he had become such a fixture in front of our kitchen fire that my parents and Aunt Mercy went to meeting with only Aunty Grinnels at home to chaperon us. The children were all tucked in bed. By leaving us alone, were my kinsfolk angling for his proposal? If so, they were to be sadly disappointed, for Lorin did not speak of love to me. Something new had happened in Nauvoo!

With the return of Orrin Porter Rockwell from the Missouri prison came news of a traitor in our midst. Just the day before, Uncle Joseph had ordered forty policemen to be hired by the city of Nauvoo to ferret out the trouble. Forty! All about the city people were talking about it. Why, just a few weeks earlier some Missourians had kidnapped some Mormons, and last year they had tried to kidnap my uncle! That wasn't so easy to do in Nauvoo, for people knew who were strangers and kept an eye on them. But to have hidden traitors among us was something new to Nauvoo! Uncle Joseph had called the traitors "dough-headed fools" and "right-handed Brutuses." Everyone wondered who they could be, and several folks developed pet theories on the subject. It seemed that anyone who had ever heard ill of someone else was anxious to bring it forward to the public at this time.

"I don't think any good can come of all this talk," Lorin said. We sat before the fire on the settle, he on one end and I on the other.

"It harks back to the troublous times of Far West, Missouri," I recalled. "Many times we were betrayed by those we thought to be friends." Every time I remembered living in Far West I felt the hair rise on the back of my neck.

"Won't be that bad ever again, Lovina."

I bit my lip with worry. "It couldn't possibly be that bad. Some people were turned out of their houses with no shoes or coats in the middle of the winter. Some died. Some lost all they possessed. Some even lost their virtue."

Lorin thought on my words, then mused, "My pa was at the Haun's Mill massacre, and he survived it. The rest of our family missed that, thank God. All we suffered was a good deal of fear of the mobs. Ma said the Lord would protect us, and he did."

"The mobs were ugly and mean to us," I said. "I grew up with persecution from the time of my birth. In Far West, traitors betrayed us to the mob."

"That's not going to happen, Lovina. We have the Nauvoo Charter and the Nauvoo Legion to protect us. Set yourself at ease."

I felt assurance as I gazed into his strong eyes. "I can't bear it if the trouble starts again, Lorin. I used to lie awake nights for fear. I was afraid a man with a painted black face would crawl through my window," I confided.

"Put your fears away. Forty police ought to catch the traitors before any trouble comes. Did you hear what Sister Turley said?" I knew something humorous was in his mind, for a twinkle came into his eye.

"No."

"She said they were those two roosters that got under the fence and mixed in with her hens. Turned traitor."

I laughed till I cried over the idea of the police looking for two roosters, due to my emotions being all tied up in knots. Then I offered Lorin some warm apple cider stewing near the coals. I drew it with a ladle and poured it into our best clay cups. We drank deeply and settled back on the bench comfortably, like two old friends.

"Did you hear that Brother Phelps wrote a New Year's hymn?" Lorin asked, making conversation after a few quiet moments while we sipped our cider.

"No, I hadn't heard. Do you know it?"

"Don't know that I'll learn it. It has no rhyme—sounded mighty peculiar!"

"I suppose that would."

A few moments later he said, "Did you hear we also have a King Agrippa in our midst?"

"As well as a Judas? It sounds as if the people of the Bible are coming back to life," I laughed.

"Sure does. That Jackson fellow was being preached to yesterday by Brother Joseph and Dr. Bernheisel, and said he was 'almost persuaded to be one with them,' unwittingly quoting Agrippa. Brother Joseph replied, 'I would to God you were not only almost but altogether,' thus quoting Paul's answer.

"What a fine thing that would be if he were baptized!"

"Oh, would it? Does that mean you would let him dance you under the kissing ball?"

"If he were one with us, he would dance no girl under the kissing ball."

An uneasy silence pursued the subject of the kissing ball. We were very much alone. I could hear the clock ticking and a child turning over in his bed. Outside, the cold wind whistled between the buildings and across the top of the chimney.

"My folks should be home soon," I said into the crackling silence.

"And if they find me still here, they'll read all sorts of meanings into it."

I stood up to stir the cider, though it needed no mixing. I wondered if Lorin meant to talk about those meanings.

"I'd better go," he said.

I looked up at him. "I suppose you must."

"I suppose I must."

"I'll get your coat." Suddenly I was afraid to let him stay any longer. Shyness overpowered me. I helped him into his coat with trembling hands. Aunty Grinnels was dozing in the other room, and I could hear her snores rising and falling evenly.

"Lovina . . ." he began.

I knew not what to do or say! I looked all around me and pulled at my hair ribbon. I felt so terribly unprepared. How did a girl respond? Should I say "Yes?"—or perhaps flutter my eyelashes? And, more importantly, was I ready to make a commitment like that?

When I hesitated, Lorin said, "Goodnight, Lovina."

The moment passed and I looked up. Oh, dear! My opportunity was over. Maybe I did want him to propose. "Goodnight, Lorin," I whispered, extending my hand. Lorin took it in his glove and kissed the tips of my fingers. Then he quickly disappeared through the door.

I thought of the verse,

He is handsome,
He is shy,
And I'll love him
Till I die.

Yes, Lorin was also shy. I ran back to the bench by the fire and held my hand before me. It was sacred! I would cover it with a glove forever. Imagine . . . Lorin's first kiss! It was a moment I would treasure for all the eternities and evermore.

When my family came home, I was still before the fire. They came into the house talking.

"Do you think we should walk over and see if they are sick and have a need, Hyrum?" Mother said while hanging her shawl on the peg.

"William looked fine when I saw him earlier. Can't think

what's happened," Father replied.

"William and Jane Law weren't at meeting this evening," they explained to me. "Have you heard anything?"

Of course I hadn't heard. My mind was still consumed by my tingling fingertips. I answered with a simple "No," and went off to bed where my thoughts could remain undisturbed.

Chapter Six

A few days later, all our thoughts were agitated when William Law told Father that he heard the forty policemen were secretly sworn by Uncle Joseph to put him out of the way in three months! We were all aghast to think that our own neighbor would say such a thing. Uncle Joseph would never want to kill an enemy, much less Brother Law, who was his neighbor and friend! Lorin was right: no good thing could come of all the gossip and speculation that were rife in the city. When such a man as William Law was suspect, it was taking things way too far. Gossip is the seed of all evil and ought to be put down.

William Law was second counselor in the First Presidency, an officer in the Nauvoo Legion, and a prominent businessman in Nauvoo. His son Richard was in our home or the Mansion every day playing with my brother John, his cousin Joseph, and Lorin's brother Henry. His wife borrowed eggs from us and nursed us with rasberry tea when we were sick. Uncle Joseph would never even think such a thing of William Law. Neither could we. However, it did explain the Laws' absence at the meeting on Saturday night.

By Wednesday, William Law and Uncle Joseph were in court over the situation. After living through betrayals at Kirtland, Independence, and Far West, Uncle Joseph was going to stop the problem with legal evidence before it grew. But it just didn't stop growing.

"All the parties parted as friends, on the surface," explained Father during dinner that evening after the younger ones had been dismissed. "But actually, this is serious. William has broken his covenants."

"What do you mean, Papa?" I asked, putting my fork down.

"The covenants of the temple have been given only to the leaders of the Church, and Brother Law has broken his. I am not at liberty to reveal details, daughter, but when I say this, your mother and Aunt Mercy understand."

"This is serious indeed," declared Aunt Mercy.

I wondered how serious it was as I prepared for bed that night. Lorin had not come to visit me that day. I had not even seen him out the window. I suspected there was a great deal of excitement over the Laws at the Mansion.

My suspicions proved well founded. The next afternoon, Emily and Eliza Partridge were at my door in a most dreadful state. They looked as if they had geen crying for several days, for their faces were mottled and bloated. I once read that red eyes caused by anything but grief or its kindred were scandalous-looking affairs. I hoped their red eyes were not caused by grief and was smitten with remorse, for in my first throes of love I had scarcely given thought to feminine company.

"Oh, Lovina!" They fell upon me, their tears soaking into my apron. "We h-have to leave Nauvoo."

"What is this? It isn't possible," I replied in disbelief, pushing them away from me so I could read their faces.

"Tis only too true. Such evil has befallen us," they wailed.

At all the commotion, the family came running. It seemed that Mother and Aunt Mercy were aware of the circumstances—and I, their dearest friend, was not! What kind of a friend was I? The two girls flew to the comfort of Mother's and Aunt Mercy's arms and wept for what seemed to me, in my bewilderment, an unendurable length of time.

"Girls!" said my brother John in disgust. He left the room, taking Joseph F. with him. "Are they going to be all right, Mama?"

my little sister Sarah asked. She was tugging at Mother's skirts. As Mother was busy, I took her up in my arms.

Mother comforted Eliza and Emily, saying, "There, there, it will all come out right in the end. The Lord at times sees fit to try us to our utmost."

"Happy times will come again when this passes," Aunt Mercy added.

"I don't see how!" cried Emily, dabbing at her eyes with her wet handkerchief.

"Me neither!" sniffled Eliza.

"I will have Brother Hyrum fix things," said Mother firmly. "Lovina, you have been patient; and now I wish to try your patience further. Mercy and I wish to have a private conversation with your friends. They are in need of a woman's counsel."

I left the room with my sisters in even greater perturbation. What counsel? Was I a child, who could not be told? After all, they were my friends! My bosom friends. Why could I not listen? I went off to my bedroom, where I picked up the dress and bedclothes I had left lying on the floor and hung them on the wall. It was very cold in my room. Hugging a shawl about my shoulders, I stared out the window at the empty Nauvoo House wharf and the lonely, icy river beyond. A lone bird flew over the frozen brown rushes. How I would miss my friends! The world would be a dreary place without their constant companionship.

Suddenly I couldn't bear it. I jumped into my bed and huddled under the quilts, shivering. Were frightening times coming again? Would I too be sent away for some unforeseen reason?

When Eliza and Emily came upstairs to me, they were in relatively better looks. Their tears had dried.

"Brother Hyrum may be able to solve our difficulties to some extent by finding us accommodation in Nauvoo. He has gone over to arrange things," Eliza explained.

"What did Mother say? Here, come get under the quilt and confide in me."

Though they each came under a corner of the quilt, they were unable to enlighten me. Forbidden.

You must tell me! You must! I will die of curiosity!" I protested, hitting the coverlet with my hand. "Have I ever proved an untrustworthy friend?"

"Lovina, do you confide all the secrets of your heart?" Eliza asked.

"Well, no," I admitted grudgingly. "No, I don't."

Patiently Eliza said, "We are not at liberty to reveal all of ours either, but do not let that diminish our friendship. That which we might share, we do."

"Might you share but one small part?" I begged. I could not bear to be ignorant when Mother knew.

Eliza said, "Everything at the Mansion is at sixes and sevens due to the defection of William Law. So concerned is Brother Joseph that he plans to rent the hotel to Ebenezer Robinson. That is best because it is too much work for Sister Emma and Olive, not to mention Brother Joseph, who must run the whole town."

I asked, "Is that all? Can't you work for Brother Robinson?"

"No."

"Whyever not?"

"That we may not share," said Eliza with amazing firmness.

Emily touched her sister on the arm, saying, "There is one part which we were afraid to tell her mother. Can't we just tell her about J. J., Eliza?"

"I suppose we might."

"J. J.? What is J. J.?" I begged, glad to be told the part Mother did not know. I felt they were my friends again.

"If you really promise and keep this to yourself," said Eliza. I nodded vigorously, and she began that part of the tale. "J.J. is Joseph Jackson. He has been hanging after me for this past month, and his attentions have increased to the extent of his becoming seriously interested in joining the Church."

"With . . ." Emily began.

"Don't say it, Emily! You'll regret it all your life. 'Tis not good to speak ill of anyone."

"Oh, go on! I can't bear this suspense," I cried, pulling the cover up to my chin.

Eliza continued while Emily kept her palm over her mouth to avoid temptation. "Mr. Jackson has become so pointed in his attentions that I fear if Brother Hyrum can arrange for us to stay in Nauvoo, and certain parties are appeased, Joseph Jackson will continue his pursuit. It could prove disastrous."

"If he repents and joins with the Saints, how can that be so great an evil? Do you care for him?" I asked.

Emily burst out, "No! She doesn't! It would cause no end of trouble! One cannot imagine!"

"He didn't get you under that kissing ball on Christmas Day, did he?" I asked. Really, I should have been paying more attention to my friends lately!

Eliza answered, "I'm afraid so. It did not help my case for staying at the Mansion to work. And I'm afraid I may not be able to avoid him in the future. Mr. Jackson is most persistent. In short, even if Brother Hyrum does arrange for us to stay with families in Nauvoo, we dare not! That is all I can tell you."

"And I shall wither and die if we leave!" wailed Emily again. "All my dreams would be destroyed, and all my youthful pleasures curtailed."

"'Twould be a bit hard to bear," admitted Eliza with a sigh.

"I should die of inutterable sorrow if you go away completely," I cried.

We spent some few moments blubbering, until the most marvelous idea came to me of how to save them. "I have a plan," I announced, "that will enable you to stay in Nauvoo."

Eliza sniffled, "No, 'tis impossible and we must resign ourselves."

"Hush your crying! I can't talk!" I scolded. When they had quieted I said, "Answer this one thing. If Joseph Jackson's affections were placed elsewhere, could you remain safely in Nauvoo, Eliza?"

"I believe I might. Yes, I could."

"Are his affections for you of a lasting nature?"

Shaking her head firmly, Eliza declared, "Oh, no, not his affections. You saw how he kissed Sarah Rigdon on Christmas. He is the most awful flirt for a former priest."

"Then you think his affections might easily be transferred to another?"

"Possibly . . ."

"Then we shall find a substitute and arrange for them to spend time together!" I declared with great enthusiasm. Joseph Jackson was not like the usual young men in Nauvoo, for his countenance and dress were very elegant. His manners exemplified one who knew his way about the world and had seen quite a lot of it. He was intelligent and appeared quite learned. In short, once he had shaken off the robes of his former priesthood, he never lacked for feminine company.

"Lovina! You are ingenious!" exclaimed Emily, all in favor of my plan. She jumped up and down on her corner of the bed, nearly oversetting herself. "It will be the saving of us!"

"Who might be the substitute?" asked Eliza quietly.

"Yes, who?" asked Emily after she had righted herself.

That question necessitated some powerful thinking.

"Sarah Rigdon?" I suggested.

"Oh, no, she's much too obvious. Mr. Jackson is a man who likes a challenge," said Eliza. "She would not succeed."

"That is why he takes to Eliza so," Emily explained. "She does not encourage him." Then, holding her hands to her cheeks, she squealed, "Oh! Oh! I have it!" She put out both her hands to us. "Remember the Christmas dance? He was quite taken with Lovina after she refused him a dance. He may perceive her as a challenge."

"Me?" I cried.

"Oh, yes! He was quite angry, so he cannot be indifferent to you," argued Emily.

"My goodness! I had not thought of myself being the decoy. Could I do such a thing? Would I care to?"

"Who would be better? Every young man in Nauvoo practically

covets your hand!" Emily said. She had completely thrown off her former languor.

"That is only because of my church connections to the Smiths. A gentile such as Mr. Jackson would not have those aspirations."

But Emily argued her case. "You underrate your attractions, Lovina. Why, if you were to but smile at Joseph Jackson, he would become your slave."

Eliza chided her, "Now Emily, you exaggerate. Though I hesitate to ask Lovina to do it, if she did we would not be under the necessity of confiding in anyone else. Anyway, all Lovina needs to do is to distract him just a little bit. Only a little harmless interest on his part will do it, I'm sure; and I will exempt myself from his company as much as possible to hasten the process."

"I forgot!" Emily exclaimed, waving her hands. "What about Lorin? Lovina, I know you have not disclosed the affections of your heart to us, but one cannot help observing developments. Lucy tells us how Lorin comes calling nearly every day. She has great hopes of a match between you and of becoming your sister. Might not your assistance to us spoil your own romance?"

"I was not aware that any romance of mine was so apparent." I felt flustered and embarrassed that they knew about a feeling of which I was so shy. I tried not to show it.

"Oh, it isn't obvious. But one wonders," Emily assured me.

Since they had shared some of their secrets, I confided, "My own feelings are private, but I will say that if what develops is a true love, then it will withstand such a tiny flirtation for the sake of friendship. Perhaps competition will even sweeten the prize."

"Oh, Lovina, you are in love with Lorin! You admit it!" cried Emily.

I blushed and they knew.

"Oh, Emily, we daresn't ask her to jeopardize her new love," Eliza protested.

"Fiddlesticks," I said staunchly. I stood up and began to smooth the bed covers. "I want to do this for you. What are friends for if not to help one another? It will not be that great a sacrifice. He is an amiable man, and intelligent. So a short time in his company cannot be so repugnant. I may even succeed in converting him to the truth."

"If not, you must promise to repulse him as soon as we have achieved our object. Oh Lovina, you are a friend forever, with a bond that cannot be broken," said Eliza with great emotion. "You can't know how much this means to me. But I give my promise that someday you shall be glad of your small sacrifice." We sealed our friendship with affectionate hugs and tears.

Chapter Seven

Our adventure began the very next evening, January the fifth. I received a note from Emily via young Joseph, my cousin. It read: "Developments. It might interest you to know that J. has just been given a commission in the N. L. as aide to the G. and is here in the M. Would you care to join us for dinner?"

"Wait!" I called to young Joseph. Hastily I scribbled a note of acceptance for him to return to Emily. Then I hurried upstairs to put on my Christmas dress, for our campaign depended on my ability to distract Joseph Jackson that evening. Not to add that I just might see Lorin, too!

Lorin hadn't come to see me because things were busy at the Mansion again. The day before, more trouble had developed. Once again there were comments by the police reported to Brother Law by some well-meaning person. This time Brother Marks had also been suspected. Were the police mad, suspecting the Nauvoo Stake President? (Though such traitors had come forth before. I could remember when the entire Whitmer family deserted us and many other friends had betrayed us.)

Immediately Brother Marks and Brother Law came to our house to see Father, who was known as an arbiter and a great soother of troubled waters. If anyone could settle a difficulty, it was Father; so all and sundry came to him with disputes and problems. This day was no different. All three men repaired to Uncle Joseph's house. Uncle Joseph assured his neighbors that he did not suspect them to be the traitors and had not said so to the police.

However, that night the police on river patrol lighted a large fire for warmth, as it was a bitter night—five bricks in my bed! We could see the fire down the street in front of Brother Marks's house. The next morning we heard that Brother Marks lay abed all night shivering with fear, wondering if he were the "Brutus" and thinking he'd be dead before morning. Did you ever hear such a tale of a grown man? And we had thought him so sensible.

Mother couldn't get over such a thing happening between the neighbors, and she was comforted only when Father came home from court and told her it was all a tempest in a teapot and not to worry. The imagined trouble once again was settled legally, so no one could ever in the future accuse Uncle Joseph about it.

And now, as the note implied, Mr. Jackson had been given a commission in the Nauvoo Legion. 'Twas an event-filled day!

When my toilet was complete (not so elaborate as the previous time I had worn the dress), I donned a shawl and rushed to the Mansion, arriving just in time for family worship. Lorin was as delighted to see me as I was him. Though yet dressed in his working clothes, he took my hand in his and bowed over it in a courtly manner. His sister Lucy was much impressed and lifted her brows. I felt the veriest traitor to Lorin with my object of interesting another man in the back of my mind.

Lorin led me to a seat next to him on the velvet settee. Grandmother came in and took a chair. Uncle Joseph entered with Mr. Jackson and a Mr. Eaton. They were engaged in a debate about politics and hardly saw me. The rest of the household followed, the children scampering to claim their favorite seats upon Uncle Joseph's lap or feet or leaning on his great shoulders. Those who were too late sat upon the floor or on the lap of their second most favorite adult. It was always thus with Uncle Joseph. I knew, for I too had once rushed to be first on his lap. Now that I was a young lady, I had other desires; and that day I had won my favorite seat—next to Lorin on the settee. It seemed, however, that I was to share this privilege, because his youngest sister, Mary, lost her race and crawled upon Lorin's lap. She placed her little arms around his neck and held him tightly as if to ward me off. Perhaps she was wiser than I that night and knew I held the power to harm his heart, though in truth I did not desire to do so. That was my last wish.

We all listened while Uncle Joseph read to us from the Book of Mormon. The words fell from his lips like sweet drops of dew distilling upon our souls. To hear the words from one blessed to personally know those of whom he was reading brought a life and a love to the story that none other could give.

Secretly I watched Mr. Jackson. Could he not feel the Spirit of the Lord that was present? How could he resist that spirit and the urge to jump up and be baptized at once? Might he not demand that we cut a hole in the river for him to be buried in its depths and come forth to a new life? I could never understand how one could resist Uncle Joseph's great and noble spirit. If I were Mr. Jackson, I would be baptized instantly! However, Mr. Jackson appeared to be testing us, trying our faith with his mind and not his spirit, his dark eyes studying each one of us in turn to see how much we believed what we heard. He had a very disconcerting eye and a cynical tilt to his brow. I felt his stare rest upon me, but I was not ashamed, for I believed the gospel with all my heart. I knew.

Gathering my wits, and with pleading looks from both Emily and Eliza, I raised my gaze at last to Mr. Jackson's; and by dint of much courage, I held his eye unashamedly. Immediately a tiny flame of interest seemed to kindle his expression, whereupon I placed my fan before my face and looked away with great modesty.

My heart pounded with fear. Had Lorin seen me stare so boldly at another man? However could I do this to him? Was my friendship with Eliza and Emily worth this? Lorin's love for me was so new and trusting, and I did not care at all for Joseph Jackson! In truth, Jackson's bold looks made me shiver with apprehension.

Then, remembering the great plight of my trusting friends and my promise to them, my heart took hold. As I listened to the stirring words of Captain Moroni, I determined to see this thing done whatever the cost to myself personally. I too was at war. I was fighting for the cause of friendship.

When he had finished reading, Uncle Joseph laid down the book and taught us, "Defense of home, family, friends, and God are the only noble reasons for war. And when these are threatened, we must stand as guardians—with our lives, if all else fails." Then he looked both Mr. Jackson and Mr. Eaton in the eye and said, "See that you remember them—home, friends, and God—these three noble reasons."

We then began to sing one of my uncle's favorite songs, "Wife, Children and Friends":

The soldier, whose deeds live immortal in story,
Whom duty to far distant latitudes sends,
With transport would barter whole ages of glory
For one happy day with wife, children, and friends.
Though valor still glows in his life's waning embers,
The death-wounded tar who his colors defends
Drops a tear of regret, as he, dying, remembers,
How blessed was his home with wife, children, and friends.

'Twas a sad song and wrought greatly upon myself and my friends. I believe we all felt like the soldier being torn from home, family, and friends. Indeed, we were all weeping into our handkerchiefs at the end of it. Even Mr. Jackson dropped his cynical look a trifle.

"Come now, we can't have these sour faces and sad countenances," said Uncle Joseph in his heartiest voice while lovingly pinching the cheeks of each child. "Answer me this conundrum: If two can play at aces, how many faces?"

"I know, I know," said young Joseph. "Three!"

"You have to answer with a rhyme, Joseph," said Julia, his older sister, aged twelve to his eleven.

Young Joseph screwed up his face so tightly that we all laughed, immediately banishing our woeful countenances.

"Someone else answer!" complained Julia.

Joseph Jackson entered the fun, saying, "The card is but a spade, two faces only are bade."

No one knew what to say. We each looked at one another significantly. Was he a gambler? He was talking about card games while we were not.

But Uncle Joseph, laughing, responded, "The game is not the same, what faces can you name?"

To cover the awkward moment, Aunt Emma quickly joined in with an answer. "The faces that you see, could be two or three, depending on your skill, could be very man-ee!"

I remembered how during the summer we pitched quoits at stocks in the evening. Crowds gathered to see the best men throw the rings. At Aunt Emma's solution we all laughed, and the air was cleared.

Mr. Jackson hastened to add, lest we think ill of him, "I assure you that I had forgotten the game of quoits in which you engage. I am but a newcomer of less than a year and was only telling you of cards from observations made on riverboat trips. I assure you that I do not participate in card games."

I wondered. So, apparently, did the others—Lorin, for one. He looked as though he could whisk me and his sisters right from the room. I thought Lucy would start to giggle about it. However, Aunt Emma smoothed the ruffled waters lest Mr. Jackson be offended. "I'm sure one cannot help what one sees," she said. "We must teach you the game of aces come spring."

"I would be much obliged, Mrs. Smith."

On that note we adjourned to dinner.

During the next week I received another message that read: "J. is now at the M. and will be leaving in about an hour."

I contrived to go on an errand to Fuller's Drug Emporium on Main Street, which was most convenient, the establishment being but a few doors further from Snyders', where Mr. Jackson was boarding. The errand proved most expeditious, for Mr. Jackson and I engaged in amiable conversation for the length of time it took to perambulate two blocks. Twirling my muff and taking small steps, I prolonged that walk as long as possible!

Another time a note came that Mr. Jackson was to remain at home for the day, and I was able to accomplish an errand right into Snyder's house. Thank the Lord for the Penny Fund! It did seem as if God were aiding Eliza's and Emily's prayers. Mr. Jackson gallantly offered to escort me throughout the rest of my labors for the temple, during which I was able to teach him of the importance of that building. It seemed as if I was also able to almost convert him to the true gospel of Jesus Christ; at least he contributed quite a few pennies to my purse that day.

I was in his vicinity as often as my tasks would allow me— not that I dared allow him to suspect, not for a moment! Not once did I behave in a forward manner towards him; but by putting myself constantly within his view, I sought to divert his interest from Eliza. Thus, by means of propinquity, we were able to feel at last that we might attain our objective.

In due course, Eliza went to stay with the family of Brother Joseph Coolidge, and Emily was taken in by Sister Sylvia Lyons—both in Nauvoo. So I was not completely cut off from my bosom friends, and we felt that the Lord was indeed merciful to us. I was glad to be able, in part, to make that possible. In the spring, when the weather warmed enough for us to get about more, I enjoyed their society quite often.

Chapter Eight

That Mr. Jackson came out today to help the brethren."

"Oh, did he? I hoped he would do so," I answered Lucy nonchalantly while we were cutting potatoes for soup in the Mansion kitchen. We were serving oceans of soup to the hungry men chopping wood for Uncle Joseph. Two hundred brethren had volunteered with fifty wagons to haul the cuttings from Mormon Springs, north of town, to the yard of the Mansion. It took a mountain of wood to heat the Mansion, and hungry work made hungry men. The loaded wagons began arriving by nine on the Mansion clock.

Lucy and I worked by the window where we could stand and view the wagons and, of course, offer our commentary on them. Such diversion for the sisters had not been possible for weeks due to inclement weather conditions, and now we were making the most of it by sharing news, recipes, and bits of advice. In the midst of this Lucy and I kept the others apprised of each arriving wagon.

"Another wagon is here!" Lucy called. "It's Brother Richards!" Then, turning to me, she continued our previous conversation. "What have you to do with Mr. Jackson?" she inquired.

Though my trusted friend, this was Lorin's sister. Dare I confide in her? Would she not be prejudiced in his interests? I concluded to answer, "Not too much," which was true enough! "He came to our home yesterday to hear Father preach, and I suggested that he join the men in service today. I am pleased that he took my advice."

"Brother Richards is coming inside!" Lucy reported and sat down. Then she said to me, "I'm glad that is all there is to it. When I saw him walking with you several days ago, I became concerned." Then Lucy lowered her voice and leaned close. "You see, I have every anticipation of you and I becoming sisters someday through Lorin, and would not want anything at all to spoil that pleasure."

I could barely answer, for my heart was in my throat. But the expression on my face was revealing enough. Lucy could tell where my true affections lay. We reached out our arms across the potatoes and sealed our mutual hopes with an affectionate embrace. Wiping the tears from my lashes with the edge of my apron, at last I answered, "If it is the will of God, may our cherished hopes of sisterhood someday be realized. It would above all things be delightful. I would wish for no other sister. But we must also see what Lorin wishes."

"I am *most* certain of his wishes! I only wished to be certain of yours."

We heard another rumbling in the yard and stood to see who was coming. "Another wagon has arrived!" I called. "Lucy, look who is on it!" I grabbed her arm. Verily, they were all of our favorites— Horace Whitney, Garrett Ivins, William Cutler, and Andrew Cahoon. After informing the rest of the kitchen of this development, we proceeded to watch the men work by abandoning our own. The young men worked hard. The stack of wood grew steadily, like the Great Wall of China.

"Here comes yet another load!" chimed Lucy.

"Another! You girls had better start chopping potatoes and stop watching the young men!" said our neighbor, Sister Turley, who had come to help and visit.

"Yes, sister," we meekly agreed.

But how could we do something so mundane as chop potatoes when on this wagon came Sylvester Emmonds, Mr. Eaton, and Joseph Jackson himself? There was no end of things to observe and comment upon, especially when Andrew Cahoon accidentally knocked Mr. Jackson with the end of a log! We were most curious when all our young men put down their wood and stood ranged against Joseph Jackson, Sylvester Emmonds, and Mr. Eaton. Would that we could hear what was said! Lucy and I pressed our noses right against the glass in the most unladylike manner. Apparently the conversation became heated and words flew, for before we knew it a fight had begun.

"Potatoes! We need more potatoes!" Sister Turley called. And when we did not comply, she bustled to our side to see what held our interest. "There's a fist fight out there!" she called in great agitation.

However, by the time the other sisters reached the window, the fight was over. It was brief, but had lingering consequences. Mr. Eaton restrained Joseph Jackson, while Andrew Cahoon was held back by William Cutler. After some arbitration, they all trooped indoors for some soup.

"I hope they settled that Jackson fellow for good," said Lucy. "The upstart!"

"Whatever do you mean?" I asked her. "It appears as if Brother Cahoon began the dispute."

"Lovina, don't you know they were fighting over you?"

"Me? However can you possibly think that?" Embarrassed, I began to chop potatoes again.

"Lovina, weren't those boys once your beaus?"

"At one time or another they all came to call on me," I admitted.

"Well, once they all realized that you were partial to my brother Lorin, they stopped calling, didn't they?"

I stopped chopping and thought hard. "Why, I suppose they did."

"They all did so with the spirit of sacrifice. Now, don't you think they should ask Mr. Jackson to do the same?"

Many thoughts raced through my mind! Forgetting the potatoes, I let several drop to the floor. Was Lucy's speculation correct? If so, would the advice of my former beaus blight his interest and return it to Eliza? What did the fight portend?

The men went about their business again and the wagons were emptied. However, the rivalry between the younger men was not over, for a race was on! At the shot of a gun, the two wagons were off. Several of the sisters came to the window to watch.

"Oh, I hope that Mr. Jackson's wagon does not win!" Lucy said in defense of her brother. I myself did not know what to hope, and I wrung my apron with my fingers.

Then old Sister Durphy came downstairs, pulling her hairpins in and out and moaning, "Oh, trouble, how it comes! This time it's that Francis Higbee. May his esteemed father, who has gone to his maker, never know of his doings!"

"Whatever has happened now, Sister Durphy?" the sisters asked. Lucy and I turned from our posts by the window to hear her news.

"Friday a week, Brother Joseph warned the young men of Nauvoo not to take Brother Francis Higbee for an example. He told them to withdraw from his society."

"We all know that," a sister answered. "What has he done now?"

Whereupon Sister Emma said, "Sisters, Wednesday's issue of the Neighbor contained a cure for the common disorder of the mouth called *scandal.* The symptoms are a violent itching of the tongue and roof of the mouth when you are in company with a species of animals called *gossips.* When you feel a fit of the disorder coming on, take a teaspoonful of the herb called *mind your own business* and hold it in your mouth, which you must keep closely shut till you get home."

For some several minutes, silence reigned in the kitchens; and every one of us experienced the most violent form of the said disorder. We dared not ask in Aunt Emma's presence.

At length our information was gleaned from a visit to the kitchens by Lorin, who brought it from the men. My, the gossips were about that day! It seemed every opinion and piece of news that had been cooped up for the winter came out for the wood-chopping and aired itself to the ringing of the axes.

Francis Higbee was suing my Uncle Joseph for speaking against him. Could you imagine him not taking reproof from the Prophet and suing for it? My, he was proud! And we gained the additional information that Uncle Joseph was in his turn suing Francis Higbee.

I hid my work reddened-hands under a corner of my apron so Lorin could not see how ugly they were.

Lorin was work-stained, too—wet and mud-covered and a bit stale-smelling. But he was a welcome sight for my eyes and his information a fitting reward for our labors. He leaned over his sister Lucy with brotherly ease and stole a handful of sliced potatoes from her lap, all the while teasing us about the sisters' easy work. I felt that he smiled extra specially for me that day, which made me wonder which wagon had won the race.

Lucy, not so reticent with Lorin as I, asked outright about the race and relieved me of my last burden of curiosity.

"Why, the brethren won, of course!" Lorin answered.

Lucy dug her elbow into my side.

I could not bring myself to look up at him after that, being much too overcome with embarrassment as I remembered Lucy's supposition about the reason for the fight. And presently Lorin returned to work.

Then Lucy said, "See, I told you they wouldn't let that Mr. Jackson win! You have nothing to worry about now."

Unknown to Lucy, I was very worried about Eliza and determined to seek out Emily and Eliza at the earliest convenient moment. I hoped Mr. Jackson had thoroughly lost interest in her, for surely he would now lose interest in me.

I continued to cut the potatoes.

Chapter Nine

Three evenings later a cotillion was held at the Mansion to relieve the tedium of January, and I was able to see for myself what effect the loss of the race had upon Joseph Jackson. I feared he would return to his pursuit of Eliza. Once again I donned my best dress and Christmas collar and arranged my tresses in English ringlets.

The dance was well attended, and while not so well decorated as the party on Christmas Day, it was graced by the music of the Quadrille Band.

I danced first with my Lorin, and secondly with Joseph Jackson. So Mr. Jackson was determined not to forsake me! That was good. However, Lorin's friends, on witnessing Mr. Jackson's continued interest in me, contrived to take him away at the close of our set of dances on the flimsy pretext of reading a letter from the Whig candidate for the Presidency of the United States concerning redress for the treatment of the Mormons in Missouri. Not that I was concerned any less than anyone else in Nauvoo about regaining our lost property and bringing the wrongdoers to justice, but it was a social evening! I thought the timing of their concern to be highly inappropriate. Men!

How was I supposed to help Eliza when all of my male friends were working against our cause? They were destroying our plot, and I could not tell them to stop. I could not even confide in Lorin.

Lorin felt free to confide in me, readily admitting to the mutual scheme to abscond Mr. Jackson. I knew not whether to feel gratification or exasperation. But I could not stay mad at Lorin for long, seeing how delighted he was to have me to himself. So after a few moments of reproof, I consented to be his partner once again.

Of course Lucy winked as she passed me with her partner, causing me to wonder if the plan was hatched by the boys or if it were the machinations of the mind of one Lucy Walker! She was most anxious to have me in the family and quite capable of it. Probably it was a bit of both.

I enjoyed two dances with Lorin before the boys came back with Mr. Jackson. They appeared to be on the best of terms and carried forth a jolly political debate, during which the boys each in turn partnered me. My feet barely stopped moving before they were dancing again. I had no opportunity to refuse my many partners or to debate their intentions. At length their behavior aroused the suspicions of Mr. Jackson, as he was quite crowded out despite his name being placed on my dance card. I could see that he was beginning to take offense. Concerned lest he mistake their actions as a representation of the behavior of Mormons, I took the opportunity to lecture each of my partners on charity towards the gentiles.

Thumping my partner on the shoulder with my fan, I said, "Brother Whitney, you cannot tell me that all of you young men are this anxious to dance with me. I will not accept that explanation."

Horace Whitney affirmed, a bit too casually, "No, none of us care to dance with you. I'll admit it. We'd rather dance with the other girls."

I stopped moving. "How dare you say that?"

Brother Whitney stopped also. "Lovina, make up your mind. First you are angry because we are giving you a whirl, and now you are angry because we aren't. You can't have it both ways."

"I think you are all behaving despicably," I declared.

"We are, aren't we?" he said with a laugh.

After that I determined to refrain from dancing at all, and I sat down in a chair on the sidelines. Mr. Jackson immediately brought me a glass of water and an apple tart. To make up for the ill treatment he had received at the hands of Lorin's friends, I smiled most warmly upon him and invited him to take the seat at my side.

"I would be honored." He threw back the tails of his coat and sat.

It seemed that all of the efforts to separate us had come to naught, for I was quite out of charity with all the young men but Mr. Jackson and would not look at them. He seemed all the more determined to make my acquaintance.

To make conversation I asked, "Where do you hail from, Mr. Jackson?"

"I lived in Georgia for a time. Much of my life has been spent travelling. I am a wanderer," he explained.

"You have seen a great deal of the world?" I asked as I nibbled on the tart.

"A great deal, yes," he said with a cynical lift to his brow.

I took a sip of water, then suggested, "Perhaps you could settle in Nauvoo. I believe our city has no rival in all the world."

"I see you are proud of it. Though in my opinion it does not rival the cities of New York and Boston, Nauvoo has much to offer—business, cultural events, and a cosmopolitan viewpoint that small places can boast. And of course, amiable company," he said.

His tone implied my company. "I'm certain you find most of the Saints amiable," I responded, hastily taking two gulps of water.

"Most of them. However . . ." He leaned towards me.

"Oh, Mr. Jackson, let me assure you that they are all quite amiable once they know what is best for them. I promise you . . ." I was babbling.

His voice came thick and low. "Come now, you are quite the champion. Certainly your own amiable qualities quite make up for all the others put together."

He was forgetting Eliza at an alarming rate! I felt a need to put a damper on his ardor. I was not at all prepared for him to like me to that degree. No wonder Eliza found him troublesome!

"Now Mr. Jackson," I said, holding the tart between us, "I have heard that the man who flatters you is not your friend. If you yield a little to flattery, you have placed yourself on dangerous ground. If you continue to yield, you are probably undone! Therefore, I shall not yield."

At that he leaned back and began to laugh most heartily, declaring that to my list of amiable qualities I must add that of wit.

"I assure you that I was not speaking in jest," I sought earnestly to convince him. "So you may not add wit to my list of qualities. I also have several *un*amiable qualities that I seek to overcome."

"One of which must be excessive humility."

"Proper humility is a virtue."

Whereupon we were once again interrupted, this time by Marcellus Bates, who exclaimed, "Just the subject with which I am most concerned! Virtue! What are the virtues of each individual? Phrenology is the means to tell all—to reveal the secrets of the soul and the mind!"

Breathing a sigh of relief, for it must be confessed that Mr. Jackson was a bit too much for me to handle, I wondered what the boys were about now. Would they dare to steal me away to have the bumps of my head examined?

Brother Bates declared, "I have only just had my skull examined and have discovered several qualities which I never knew I possessed."

"I could tell you several," I offered sarcastically. He was overdoing his part.

Joseph Jackson laughed again, then whispered to me, "I was correct in my supposition that you are a comic."

By now I was quite out of patience with all the young men, including Mr. Jackson, and despite my promise to Eliza was quite ready to depart his company, too.

Before I could do so, Brother Bates said, "Horace Whitney has lately taken up the science of Phrenology and is studying our bumps. Would you like your personality revealed, Mr. Jackson?"

"Perhaps it will flatter you," I suggested demurely.

Joseph Jackson laughed again at my remark, slapping his pantaloons twice. "Though perhaps not," he said. He looked a bit nervous about having his bumps read and began to finger his cravat.

"Come now, Jackson, it is the latest scientific discovery! Try it," Brother Bates said with cajolery.

"Will you mind?" he asked me.

Whereupon Brother Bates quickly said, "We will perform it right here. Ah, Brother Whitney is ready now."

At once Mr. Jackson was surrounded by several young men, which effectively shut me off from his vision. Brother Whitney began to feel his bumps. I rose and walked away from them all. However uncertain I was of the amount of science involved in this particular study of the skull, I was most certain it was done for the benefit of Lorin Walker; for, seeing me free of partners and conversation, he immediately claimed me to dance once again. It was a waltz.

"Now Lorin, did you and the boys plan that against Mr. Jackson so he could not waltz with me?"

He looked much too innocent as he placed his hand on my wrist. "Horace is crazed with this new science. We've all had our bumps read."

I found that hard to believe and rolled my eyes heavenward. "And just what did your bumps reveal?" I asked impatiently.

"That I'd dance with the loveliest girl in Nauvoo four times tonight."

Now that was a statement of pure, unadulterated flattery! But as I glanced at Lorin's face and saw that he meant every word, I knew that that form of flattery held no harm. I forgave him with all my heart.

"Did you find your analysis flattering or humbling?" I asked

Joseph Jackson at the conclusion of the evening.

He raised both his brows and flashed his dark eyes. "I find it best to live dangerously, therefore I heard only the flattery."

"Then, as was foretold, you will soon find yourself undone," I replied primly.

"Never. I live a charmed life," he whispered.

Now I raised my brows. "That must be wonderful indeed, but charms fade with time."

"Ah, I'm sure yours won't."

Now that was flattery! Flicking my fan over my face, I turned my back on Mr. Jackson and began to speak once again with Lorin. How safe Lorin was—like a welcoming harbor to come home to.

Chapter Ten

"Lovina, I would like to talk to you in my office," said Father.

I knew what it was about. For the past two nights, while he and Mother and Aunt Mercy were at Prayer Meeting above the Brick Store, I had had two gentlemen callers, one of whom he did not approve. And as I had been inadequately chaperoned under that condition, my conduct was called into question. Gentleman callers who were not approved of were usually surrounded by the family until they were smothered out.

"But there were two callers together, and Aunty Grinnels was at home," I explained. "I could not help him calling, and I could not tell him to leave!"

"I don't approve of Jackson. I would wish you to avoid the very appearance of evil, daughter. You must set the example for the youth of the Church."

"Yet you allowed Lorin and me to stay *alone* with only one chaperon," I protested (though truly I hadn't minded).

My Father gave me a benevolent smile—oh, the family matchmakers! "We approve of Lorin. We wanted to leave you alone. Lorin is something like a tortoise in his courtship."

I felt perfectly shocked at my father! He had probably told Aunty Grinnels to fall asleep. Harking back to the sweet memory of Lorin's kiss on my fingertips, I could not help revealing that Lorin had made some progress that evening. My cheeks suffused with color and I clutched my cherished fingertips tightly in my other hand. Of course the kiss had long since worn away, but its memory still lingered in my heart.

"Perhaps young Lorin is not so dilatory as I thought. Has he discussed marriage with you?" Father sat back in his chair and watched me shrewdly.

Embarrassed, I wiggled about in my seat. "Father! How can you ask such a thing? Lorin behaved like a perfect gentleman and left when Aunty Grinnels fell asleep! And last night he stayed only until Mr. Jackson departed! He may have no matrimonial intentions at all. I would be intensely mortified if you were to meddle. What would he think of me?"

At that information my father placed his fingertips together and gave me another one of his satisfied smiles. "So he was determined to wait Jackson out, was he? Good for him."

Lorin had looked awfully tired the night before last, and had come visiting in his broadcloth work shirt and suspenders. He had not even changed his tattered leather hat or heavy coat, and his boots were caked with dried mud. He had labored all day long on the temple lifting those heavy stones, and had desperately needed his sleep. Yet when Mr. Jackson seemed determined to stay, all dressed in the finest suit to be found outside of St. Louis, Lorin doggedly remained in his chair before the fire, his head nodding. It wasn't until the second candle guttered that they both took the hint to leave—together. Poor, tired Lorin!

He must have been watching again Sunday night, for he came immediately after Mr. Jackson called. He was much more rested and able to contribute a great deal to the conversation, which was upon the subject of Uncle Joseph's sermon that morning at the temple site. Well-informed on that subject, he was able to outshine the better-educated Mr. Jackson in his oratory. I believe the discussion was not very conducive to converting Mr. Jackson to the principle of sealing parents to children, for it became somewhat of a debate, with Mr. Jackson taking the opposite argument. Verily, I felt at times as if I were the conductor of the lyceum!

I remembered one topic that had been debated at the Nauvoo Lyceum that winter: "Should females be educated to the same extent as males?" All of the females ranged themselves on the side of the one selected to argue in behalf of educating females and cheered him on quite vocally. That is how I felt in this debate. I could only cheer one side.

At last Mr. Jackson gave in by quoting, "All orators are dumb when beauty pleadeth."

Father continued his lecture, and my mind returned to the present. "We do not wish you to encourage Mr. Joseph Jackson by your words or actions. He is a gentile."

"Yes, Papa." I no longer wished to encourage him either. I believed that Emily and Eliza and I had accomplished our design and that he would no longer seek her out.

"If he comes to call again, all the family will remain with you, or I myself will carry him away to the study."

"Yes, Papa," I agreed wholeheartedly.

And that is just what happened the very next night. But, as the night following that one was another cotillion, I was unable to fulfill all of my father's wishes to the letter.

I sought to be an obedient daughter. I had reason to wish to obey and seek no further friendship with him, for I was anxious to pursue my romance with Lorin. But in this effort I was thwarted on every side. My champions on the previous occasion forsook me, every one. Having filled the places on my dance card with their names, foremost among them Lorin's, they all repaired to the bar to discuss national politics and to see for themselves how the apple cider tasted now that Ebenezer Robinson had taken over management of the Mansion House.

Even Joseph Jackson went with them into the bar! So we sisters had no partners to speak of. The band played on. At length, Mr. Jackson returned with Brother James Monroe and Mr. Emmonds and stopped before our bench.

"I regret to inform you that Masters Whitney, Cutler, Cahoon, and Walker wish to excuse themselves and offer their apologies for the inconvenience to you ladies," said Brother Monroe.

This caused no small amount of consternation among the sisters!

"Have they taken ill?" Lucy asked.

Mr. Jackson cleared his throat and replied, "I believe that is the case."

I turned pleading eyes to Lucy, who had a brother among them and therefore the right to inquire after him at least. "Have they departed?" she asked.

"I believe they are unable to; and, as Mrs. Smith is an able nurse and has several male attendants in the place, they are in a chamber upstairs," replied Mr. Jackson with great politeness.

Lucy asked, "Is Lorin very ill? Ought I to inquire?"

"We hope the sickness will soon pass," said Mr. Jackson. "They may perhaps rejoin us ere the dance is over. Perhaps until then, might we offer our services? To quote Lord Byron, 'On with the dance! Let joy be unconfined.'" Whereupon he bowed before me and held out his elbow.

What was I to do? I could not be rude, despite my good intentions. So I rose and danced with him. And then yet a second time.

But I grew concerned when the young men did not return to the party. "Lucy, could you inquire after Lorin and the others?" I whispered when I returned to my chair. Though it would be indelicate to ask for details, I wished to know how ill they were.

While she was gone, Sylvester Emmonds partnered me. As he too was a gentile, I felt my evening a poor success. Whatever would I tell my father?

At length, Lucy returned with the news that Lorin was abed and could not return. The others had departed for home, feeling well enough only to do that.

"Will you inform me of his progress?" I begged Lucy as I also departed. The evening had proved a great disappointment to me.

She placed her cheek against mine affectionately and whispered, "If you were already engaged, you would have the right to see for yourself!"

Embarrassed, I turned quickly away and left. Yes, I did wish I had that right and was tightly bound to him by promise. I wished it over and over during the next few weeks, for Lorin did not recover quickly. I learned from Lucy that he bore symptoms of quinsy and was wracked by ague and fever. Some wanted to have his blood let, and another brought him a remedy of chimney soot boiled in water and mixed with cream and sugar. Still another brother suggested opening his bowels with senna and salts. Uncle Joseph would allow none of this, and Aunt Emma fed him with herb mixtures. His brother William spent hours sponging his fevered brow with cool water. Indeed, at times his life hung in the balance.

Would that we could return to that evening beside the fire, with Aunty Grinnels gently snoring in the other room! How differently I would respond! Instead of turning away so modestly to stir the cider which needed no stirring, I would lift my eyes to his gentle hint! And if he kissed my fingertips, I would hold his hand firmly and keep it there! Always to hold! Oh, why was it that only Lorin made me shy?

Chapter Eleven

Lucy was my lifeline that week. She came almost hourly with a report on Lorin's progress. It was slow. Indeed, I hardly noticed that Joseph Jackson came to call each evening during the week that followed the second cotillion. True to his word, Father took him into his study or out with him on his business. If Father was not home, Mr. Jackson was soon smothered by my sisters and brothers and womenfolk. We spake nary a word together. I was blessedly left in peace with my private concerns and tender moods.

Even the electrifying, sensational news that my own Uncle Joseph Smith had become a candidate for President of the United States did not move me to joy or relieve my anxiety for Lorin, though the news lighted the town like a prairie fire. "Now we will get redress from Missouri!" "The Prophet will set 'em all straight in Washington!" "Just think how this will spread the gospel abroad throughout the land!" "Now we'll see how America takes to the true gospel of Jesus Christ!" "We will set up a standard to the nations of the earth—a model of true democracy!" "May Nauvoo become the empire seat of government!" And many more such comments were made by the well-wishers and visitors who came to call at our house.

Among our callers, early the day after the announcement, when Lorin had been sick one full week, Joseph Jackson came—in this instance for the purpose of a private interview with my father.

I had at one time bemoaned those suitors who besought shirt-tail salvation by means of marriage to me. And now Father said that I had one who sought shirt-tail sensationalism through marriage to me! For verily, the worldly, debonair, never-to-settle-down Joseph Jackson sought my hand in marriage. This phenomenon took me so much by surprise that I was at last shaken from my lethargy and concern for Lorin! I shook my head and wondered what had come over Jackson? I had given him little reason to believe I felt affection for him or that our viewpoints were compatible. And surely he was not overtaken by my supposed charms to the extent that he would end his wandering and bind his destiny to mine. His feelings could not possibly be that strong or be based on love or affection, for they had proved to have no lasting value in the case of Eliza. His motivation could only be his desire for consequence.

My father, when he had time to devote to my inquiries, made me privy to the fact that Joseph Jackson had not only asked for my hand, but had threatened my father with revenge at his refusal! My, he was determined! I confess that for a few weak moments I felt it most gratifying to be wanted to such a degree, even if not for love; for Mr. Jackson was an educated, handsome, and exceptionally well-dressed man, and had never before offered for a female. But on the whole, his interest proved most worrisome. I had never thought for a moment that our scheme to divert him from Eliza would work so thoroughly.

Later that day, when Lucy came to make her daily report on Lorin's progress, she had much news to impart. She took off her bonnet and pelisse and told me that Joseph Jackson had gone to Uncle Joseph for the purpose of persuading him to override my father's denial of his suit! Again Mr. Jackson hadn't taken a refusal with grace—and Uncle Joseph had gained a new enemy.

And here was poor Lorin, lying in bed so sick that he could not even be told!

"Would that he could avenge you!" Lucy cried.

"For what reason?" I asked her.

"It is said that you encouraged Mr. Jackson."

I sat down in a chair and stared at my friend in wonderment for a few moments. "I? Nothing I have done has been beyond the bounds of ordinary courtesy."

Lucy sat across from me. "It is also whispered that Lorin has not quinsy, but was poisoned."

My jaw dropped. Then I declared, "Poisoned? Whoever would poison Lorin? He has not an enemy in all the world."

"Has he not?"

"Certainly not! He is the most amiable person alive. As his sister, you should know that!"

"Jackson?" she asserted slyly.

"Surely he could not be capable of such an act!" I declared.

"Did he not threaten Brother Hyrum with revenge? Did he not tell Brother Joseph he would see to his downfall for his refusal to interfere?" Lucy argued.

I protested, "You imply a serious wrong! Think of the consequence to his reputation if such a notion became general!"

Lucy stood and gathered her things to depart. "As it can never be proven, it will remain a whisper. But I'll tell you this: the only other men to take sick in that bar room were the same ones who had played tricks on Mr. Jackson at the previous cotillion."

I became extremely suspicious as I thought over Lucy's words and added, "And they engaged in a fight at the wood chopping! Do you think . . .?"

"Yes, I strongly believe that he poisoned Lorin." She tied her bonnet strings tightly as if to emphasize her point.

"Oh! Then he is a far more dangerous man than he admitted to being! Much more so!" I began to accept her insinuations and had to sit down.

"Yes," Lucy said as she departed.

Throughout the remainder of the day, as I tended the babies and mended the linens, I thought of nothing but the disclosures made by my friend, Lucy Walker. Could the things whispered about have a sure foundation? Was Mr. Jackson capable of so vile and despicable an act? Such treachery? Was it possible to administer poison in so public a setting? And if so, with what possible motivation?

I stopped with my needle in mid-motion. Surely it could not have been for romantic love of myself! Surely a man of such worldly experience and charm, who had several young ladies languishing for his favor, would not risk so much for a few dances with a young woman such as I, a member of a persecuted people and of but average attainments and charms. To such an extent as to attempt murder? Yes, possibly murder. Never! The very idea was absolutely preposterous!

Yet, circumstances led one to suspect that it was so. It was true that he had ample cause to take offense. It was also true that his interest in me had grown proportionately to the amount of persecution inflicted upon him. It was also true that the persons supposedly infected with poison were those very persecutors. And Jackson had taken advantage of their affliction by dancing with their abandoned partners! Then he had come calling on me with a clear field ahead, Lorin out of the race. And as soon as he had realized that there might be worldly gain and recognition involved through an attachment to me, he had sought it, but not before. The circumstances were undeniable, and this was the crux of the issue—he threatened vengeance!!!

By the time I had mended three sheets and two pillowcases, I was convinced that Mr. Jackson was a veritable murderer! Fie upon him! Might his body lie moldering upon a dungheap! I was fair done with his society. I bit off my sewing thread hard.

Yet my association with him could not be undone so entirely, for there were whisperings abroad that threatened to destroy my reputation. And I did not dare to vindicate myself for the sake of my two friends for whom I had performed the service. How were Eliza and Emily and I to know that our plan would have such far-reaching effects, like an odor caught by the wind? My Lorin lay dying.

By the time the children were tucked in bed and I had prepared my own toilet, I was heartbroken, certain that I had brought suffering upon my love by my own foolish choices. Would that I could repent of them! Would that I could undo that which was done! Would that I could breathe the breath of life into his soul and that he might be healed!

Night after night I knelt at my window and pleaded with my Father in Heaven to spare Lorin's life. Each night the moon hung over the riverbanks on the western shore before I withdrew from my wrapper and gained the physical comforts of my bed, my warming bricks long since cold. I prayed each night for my love's recovery, that we might someday marry and rear children and gain the blessings of eternal life together. I came to love Lorin as I never had. Before, I had loved the way he combed his hair or the way he sat upon his horse. Now, I loved *him*. And I wanted him forever—most desperately!

Each night the moon lit up the river world, silver and frozen in time, the currents of its life held bound until the spring thaw. Each eddy and shallow first frozen by winter's air had caught the more swiftly-flowing waters and frozen them into life patterns for all to see and study. Such was my life for me to see—a pattern of tiny faults catching at the mainstreams of my existence and freezing them in time. I could see and examine each of my flaws—my vanity, my desire for the glory of the world, my hesitation to become an adult and take on the responsibility of raising children. All were revealed to me.

Oh, when would the river flow once again? Like the river, were Lorin and I to be frozen in time?

The moon grew from a tiny sliver to a full circle, and still the river—and my life—lay frozen. I thought I could not live on if Lorin did not get well. I was willing to lay my heart and soul upon the altar of sacrifice for his sake. One night, thinking upon these things, I leaned my brow against the windowsill.

At that moment, a light brighter than the moon began to fill my room. And a voice came to me, saying, "Be not troubled, for you shall have the desires of your heart. Your offering is acceptable to me. It is enough."

Oh, what joy filled the extremities of my searchings! Just to make certain the Lord understood me without question, I cried in my soul, "Give me back my Lorin! Let me be his forever! Let my desires be only those of my Lord! Thy will be done!"

And it was done. The next day Lucy came to tell me that at that same moment Uncle Joseph had anointed Lorin with holy oil, and he was healed. The devil went right out of him and he was freed. Lorin sat up and ate two bowls of chicken soup all by himself.

I cried and cried in her arms. What the Lord could do! Oh, how holy was His name! I would praise Him forevermore.

The ice began to thaw.

Chapter Twelve

In spite of my extraordinary spiritual experience, as Lorin grew in strength and was able to begin his labors once again, he did not come to call. I watched for him, but he did not come. Each night as I sat at my windowsill and looked out upon the frozen waters and noticed the ice warming and breaking up, I wondered why. Only patches and streams of water were once again caught in the swift movement of the current. Such was my life. I took it up again and went out and about, done with my mourning. Yet a part of me was still frozen, caught around the edges, waiting for the full thaw.

Was Lorin done with me? Had I hurt him irreparably? Had he heard the whisperings that were about? Had he heard idle talk that I had behaved with impropriety? Would he believe it? Was this the cause of his turning from me? Oh, that I could only know his heart and mind! On many a night, I pounded my fist against the sill in desperation.

My comfort at these times was that the Lord had heard the desires of my heart clearly and completely and had offered His undeniable assurance to me. I could but trust and wait in patience. But what of the principle of free agency? Lorin was free to choose.

With the thaw came a visit from my friends, Emily and Eliza, saying, "We have only just heard of Lorin's sickness," and in a much lower voice, "and its possible cause."

"Have the speculations been whispered about that far?" I inquired.

Eliza said, "No. We heard it from Lucy."

"That is a mercy. I feared I would become a topic for the newsmongers." I lowered my head.

"Oh, Lovina! We never envisioned that our predicament would cause you such distress!" cried Emily.

What words of consolation could I offer? My assistance had caused us much distress. Yet had I the decision to make again, I might still make the sacrifice, for they were my friends and had been in need. "Twas the right thing to do at the time," I finally said, raising my head.

"It was. But how can we undo the damage?" asked Eliza. "What damage?" I asked.

"That done to your reputation. And Lorin's illness," she said. I touched her arm and assured her, "Eliza, those who know me well know that I would never countenance marriage to a gentile. I have too great a testimony of the gospel for that. And those who know me not that well will soon see by my actions that such is the case."

"But Mr. Jackson goes about saying that you wish to wed him despite your father," she alleged.

My eyes grew large as full moons, and I sat up straight as a poker. "That I wish to wed him! How *dare* he make such a claim?"

"He told Sarah Rigdon. But we know it is untrue."

"Lorin must have heard his lies. Oh, how can he think that of me?" In my distress, I covered my face.

"Lorin?" questioned Emily.

"He has ceased to call. Truly, I have not seen him since he signed my dance card and repaired to the bar room on the night he took sick."

Eliza stood up in great agitation and began to pace the room. "He must be told the truth at once. Oh, when I think how we have wronged him, I am filled with disgust at our selfishness! You must allow us to make amends."

I protested, "What can you say to him? You must not betray my feelings. I would not like him to gain the impression that I had sent you to him on purpose to gain his affections! Perhaps he holds me in disgust. I would look too foolish!"

"I don't think 'tis so." Emily looked at Eliza. "Jane Manning said that she was often working upstairs when he was in a state, and he often called out your name. Then Jane would go in and pretend to be you and say, 'Here I is.' Lorin would then beg you not to leave him, ever."

Eliza added, sitting before me earnestly, "So we are morally certain he still loves you, whether he knows it consciously or not."

"Oh." My heart blossomed with hope. Just that morning I had seen the first spring flowers poking through the earth. They had portended only good.

"Then go to him. Quickly!" I pleaded.

Though they told him all my part against Jackson, still Lorin did not come to call. I came to believe that he did not care for me.

That was not my only trouble. Several times my brother John had sighted Joseph Jackson calling upon the Laws across the way. And as the anti-Mormon newspaper, the *Warsaw Signal*, had published a very insulting poem about Uncle Joseph, who believed it to be the work of Brother Wilson Law, William's brother, we feared that not just they, but a whole group was uniting against us when we saw Joseph Jackson visiting the Laws. William Law hadn't spoken to Uncle Joseph since January eighth! That was over a month before. Ah, the echoes of Far West came again when our friends became enemies!

Those echoes grew into clamors by Saturday, February seventeenth! The Anti-Mormon Party, formed in Hancock County to defeat the Mormons in elections, held a convention to devise ways and means to expel the Mormons from the state. It all sounded much too familiar . . .

Nevertheless, that was not what caused me to lie awake at night with tears soaking into my pillow. What did it matter if I should be bereft of home or property if I were now bereft of my singlemost desire? What did it matter that the winds of hatred were gathering against us when winds of loneliness were already raging through my heart? Where was love? Where was the joy of youth?

Yet I remained a dutiful daughter and performed all my labors well and patiently. I mended, washed the family clothes, cooked the porridge, swept the floor, tended the baby, and at times even hauled in logs for the fire. When I had opportunity, I searched the words of the Lord for consolation. I participated in family worship and attended the meetings held when weather permitted. I visited the sick and collected pennies. But I could not attend social events. I could not force myself to do so. My despondency would be apparent to all.

I called to see Grandmother Smith who lived in the Mansion, hoping for a glimpse of Lorin. Though I visited often and stayed long, I never saw my love and believed him to be avoiding me. At length I was finally rewarded for my endurance, for Lorin came a-knocking on our door and walked in. My faith, he looked a scarecrow! No wonder I had not seen him about! I would never have known him. Compared to the healthy, robust, and dashing young man with whom I had engaged to dance when I last saw him, this Lorin was somber and thin and balding. He did not smile or speak to me. He looked as if he had viewed the very portals of death and had paid for his life with his youth. He looked old. His hair had grayed at the edges, and some of it had fallen out. His eyes were like sockets in his cheeks. Where was my Lorin? Who was this stranger?

So shocked was I that instead of leaping to my feet and rushing to welcome him to our home, I remained in my chair by the fire. And before I could collect my wits, Lorin had disappeared into the office with my father.

My mending fell to the floor, ignored. I leapt up and paced about the room, wringing my hands, wondering whatever purpose this new Lorin had in coming to call on Father. I felt nigh to distraction. Was he on business for Uncle Joseph? Or, was he calling on Father for the purpose I had most desired? I wished I could see through the door.

Alternately, I wiped away a tear shed for the state of his health. How he must have suffered from his illness! No wonder he could not forgive me. My poor darling Lorin! I could not forgive myself.

"Mama, Lovina's crying," said little Martha Ann to Mother when she came into the room.

"What's the matter?" she asked anxiously.

Mary Jane, Aunt Mercy's daughter, said, "Lorin came to call on Uncle Hyrum. He looks like bones and it made Lovina cry."

"Is that it?" Mother asked me.

So much for privacy when one has personal troubles! "Yes," I confessed, "Tis the trouble." I sat down.

Mother began to smile and hum to herself as she turned the fish frying over the fire. "We'll be planning a party."

"Whatever do you mean?"

"When a young man closets himself with a father, it can only mean one thing—a proposal of marriage."

"Think you so? It could also mean business."

Mother stopped her work and looked at me as only she could. It made me remember the several times I had done something young and foolish and had been found out. "Lorin is soliciting your hand in marriage! And you'd better stop your fretting and change your dress before your father calls you in there."

Trusting Mother, I gave her a hug, then ran to change my dress, comb my hair, and sprinkle some crushed lavender on my petticoat. I glanced out of my window, noticing that the ice had left the shore of the river and that the water was rushing along its banks once again. My heart pounded in my breast. Surely that was a good sign!

"Lovina! Your father wants you in his office!" Mother called to me like a song. Her voice filled me with hope.

I hurried down the stairs. As I passed Mother, she took my hands in hers, squeezed them in encouragement and whispered, "All the grace of God is upon you in this."

"That I know," I whispered back.

Then I entered the office. Determined never to repeat my former mistake of being too shy to offer Lorin encouragement, I did not lower my eyes. Lorin lowered his. Oh dear, why could he not look at me? Was I now so displeasing to him? Father seated me and I resolved to offer a clear vision to Lorin no matter what. Never again would I discourage him.

"Lorin has something to ask of you," said Father.

Lorin cleared his throat and shuffled his feet. He moved his bony hands up and down his best suit pants. They hung upon him. At length he began. "Last night Brother Joseph had a talk with me." He shuffled his feet some more, then continued, "the Lord told him to command me to marry you."

After he said that, he looked up quickly, then down, and lapsed into silence.

I too was silent. I knew that the Lord willed it. Had I not His promise? Had He not redeemed Lorin from the jaws of death for that purpose? But, did Lorin will it? Did he love me, or was he only being obedient to command?

"What do you say, Lovina?" my father prompted.

At last I heard my voice squeak out a query. "Do you wish it, Lorin?" My lashes blinked with tears, yet still I held my gaze upon him.

Then Lorin lifted his eyes and looked into mine. He swallowed a few times. "Yes, I do."

I managed a half smile and replied, "I will marry you."

Father was overjoyed. He rose and shook our hands and led us into the kitchen to tell the family. Now I could not bring myself to look at Lorin for all the fish in the river. Yet at the same time I wanted to climb the trees along the street and shout to all and sundry the news that LORIN WANTED TO MARRY ME!

We never had a moment alone. The whole family planned the party set for Tuesday, the twentieth of February, one day hence. All the next day we cooked and cleaned and shook out our best dresses, as busy as a hill of ants. There was no time to sew a new dress for this party. But what was a new dress when I now had Lorin?

All the church leaders and their wives came to pay their good wishes to us. We stood side by side, receiving each couple as they came to call. Yet we still did not speak in private. I began to be assailed with doubts and started to fidget with my lace collar. Where were the flatterings and compliments of Lorin's former courtship? Did he still care for me? He didn't look happy to be marrying me. He no longer teased me or told me I was the prettiest girl in Nauvoo. Did this new Lorin, who looked so different and acted so sober, still love me? Had he forgotten his feverish ravings when he had called out for me?

There was no dancing that evening, so the men gathered on one side of the room and the women on the other. I strained to hear any word that Lorin might say, leaning far back in my chair, yet all I heard was talk of sending volunteers to explore the Oregon territory as a possible place for the Saints to move if Uncle Joseph was not elected President. Would Lorin volunteer? Would he be torn from my side before we had become properly acquainted? He sounded quite enthusiastic about the project. My doubts increased. Oh, that I could but talk with him alone! I kept fidgeting with my collar.

Then I heard someone say, "That Jackson fellow sure was anxious to volunteer."

"Humph," my father replied. "Wouldn't do at all."

"Brother Robinson learned from Mr. Eaton that Jackson planned to steal Lovina away when the river was clear. You'd better keep a tight eye out on her, Brother Lorin."

My blood stopped and froze within me. Quickly I lowered my eyes, for all conversation had stopped among the circle of women. I held tightly to the arms of my seat. Jackson was planning to steal me away? Was this thing true? What a horror of a fate! I could see myself squirming in his arms as my helpless family stood on the banks of the river, disappearing forever. Then I envisioned Lorin swimming out to save me. What a notion! Was that the reason why

Lorin had offered for me? To protect me from such a possibility? Jackson would not dare abduct an engaged girl. My heart cried out that this could not be true, but in my mind the doubts and fears grew out of all proportion. I could not sit still in my chair.

The talk continued. "Jackson threatened to shoot anyone who came near the skiff. Planned it with yonder Law across the way."

Father said, "I think so little of Mr. Jackson that I can believe such a threat from him. The Lord commanded Lorin to offer for Lovina just in the nick of time. Can't steal away an engaged girl and get away with it. People would know she wasn't willing. I must say that it breaks my heart for a good neighbor to betray me like William has. Can it be true?"

The brother assured him of his sources.

"I cannot believe William would wish such a calamity upon us after all our years of friendship."

At that the talk turned to the defection of Brother Law from the Church and the women once again turned to the subjects of children, gardens, and new fashions in an effort to cover the disquiet the news brought to our family. They were full of charity.

But I was shattered. I could just imagine Lorin being shot as he tried to save me. And I could imagine that was the reason that Lorin had offered. Blast Joseph Jackson and his thirst for revenge! I hoped he would drown in the river in his cursed skiff if he ever came near me. He had certainly drowned all my dreams.

Chapter Thirteen

The next morning Mother and Aunt Mercy brought out my hope chest. Regrettably, it was only half full. Much work lay ahead for me before I could be married. A girl needed a good supply of everything—bed linens, towels, dresses for day and evening, undergarments, gloves, hats, shoes, and most important, a wedding dress.

"Whatever ails you, girl?" Mother asked when I stopped looking at our fabric and stared into the corner. I was not showing the proper enthusiasm for the enterprise.

I burst into tears. As it was a warm day, Aunt Mercy bundled up the children and sent them out to play in the yard so we could talk undisturbed and privately.

They both sat down firmly before me. "Now we'll hear about it," said Mother. "Is it that you don't wish to marry the young man? No one is forcing you."

I confessed, "It's Lorin. I don't know if he loves me!"

"He asked you to marry him, didn't he? What more evidence can you ask, save an angel from heaven?" asked Mother, throwing up her hands in exasperation.

I sniffled and answered, "He only did so because he was commanded to."

Aunt Mercy came over to me and placed her arm about my shoulders. "Why, that's the best reason of all. Mary and your father married for the same reason, and look at all the happiness their union has brought to your home. Did you think your father was ready to marry so soon after the death of Jerusha? Yet he obeyed the Lord and gave you a mother."

I looked up and asked, "Did you not mind, Mother?"

She answered firmly, "I very soon had him loving me because it was right. And he still loves me and honors me. A command of the eternal God is a much surer foundation than all your frivolous notions of falling in love."

Aunt Mercy comforted, "All will be well, Lovina. You'll see. There is always happiness in obedience to the Lord."

I was not sure and remained silent. What if Lorin only married me to please the Lord? What if he didn't love me? What if he grew to resent me? What if we lived throughout eternity unhappily?

"What you need is some time alone with that young man!" said Aunt Mercy. Bless her, she understood! "Why, I remember having the same doubts when I was promised to Brother Thompson. Every young couple needs time to court and to plan. You have not had a moment."

I agreed. "That's true. Nary a word have we spoken since before his illness!"

Mother rose from her chair and found paper and a quill. "You write that young man a note and command him to take you out in the carriage. When you get him into it, make him take you clear out to the prairie and then stop. You'll soon have him talking of love. Mind you, stick to talking, though."

"Mother!"

"Though you may not believe it, I was once young and had one or two beaus in England," she said with a girlish smile.

"I remember that," said Aunt Mercy.

I liked the idea. But was it safe? Since I had heard of Jackson's boast to steal me away, I was afraid to leave the house. "But what about the threat of Mr. Jackson?" I asked.

"I said the prairie, not the river. He threatened to take you away in a skiff. Besides, you'll be with Lorin."

I would be alone with Lorin! I began to jump up and down

and ran around the room exuberantly. Would he go? Would he indeed take me out to the prairie? Would he speak the words I longed to hear? Perhaps!

At last I sat at the table and penned the letter. Never had I written to a young man before and knew not how to begin. Dearest? My Lorin? Or simply, Brother Walker?

Aunt Mercy took pity on me saying, "Lovina, just write, 'Dear Lorin,' and ask him to take you driving. Simply. Don't elaborate or he'll suspect."

"How should I sign it?"

"Lovina."

"Oh. Is that all there is to it?" And turning back to my task, I penned the note as she suggested.

"Fold it up and give it to John to deliver. If I know Lorin, he'll be here within the hour. You'd better get dressed."

And so he was! I put on my shawl. Lorin couldn't get the use of the curricle or the carriage and wondered if I would care to take a walk by the river instead.

"What about Mr. Jackson's threat to abduct me in a skiff?" I asked before we left the safety of the yard.

Lorin calmly walked through the gate and boasted, "I'm not afraid of him. Besides, he's on the other side of town."

Still I would not go out the gate. "Lorin! How do you know that? You young men have not been hectoring him again, have you?"

"A whole battalion has been after Mr. Jackson—my two brothers, Edwin and Henry, and Joseph and your brother John. They started today. Soon all the boys in the Boys' Brigade will be following him. Mr. Jackson will get no peace while he is in Nauvoo."

"But they mustn't. He may be a very dangerous man!"

"Lovina, they won't get closer than a stone's throw. I just want them to watch him so he can't bring you to any harm. Besides, they're having no end of fun doing it. Come on."

Lorin put out his arm and smiled. I took it and we began walking towards the landing. Now this was the way I liked it, just the two of us and my arm in his. I'd dreamed of just such a stroll by the river.

We skirted the landing and walked along the water's edge for about half a mile until we came to the place where the lily pads blossomed in the summer. Mother said they were like an English garden. Near the river was a log set under a sheltered ledge. I primly perched on one end and Lorin settled on the other. Two people could have sat between us on the log. We were quite alone. The only nearby sounds came from birds and insects and the lapping of the water. Lorin stood up and walked to the river's edge, then came back and sat closer. One person could fit between us now. It seemed that Lorin might have the same desire as I.

"Lovina, can I ask you a question? You don't have to answer now if you are not inclined to." He stared towards the water, not at me.

"Anything," I answered quickly.

At length he asked, "Why did you consent to marry me?"

Swiftly I looked up at Lorin, but his gaze was on the ground at his feet, where he was digging dried grasses with a stick. Could it be that he too had the same doubts?

"The Lord commanded it," I said. Oh I was craven! Where were my vows to be bold and to meet his eye unflinchingly when he hinted of love? I was bound by my own modesty. I could not even change my answer.

Lorin was silent for a time again, digging at roots. "Is that the only reason?"

I could not actually lie nor dissemble, so I asked a question in turn. I did not dare to reveal my love before he did. "Why did you ask me?"

"The Lord . . ."

I interrupted, entirely weary of this reason. "I know the Lord commanded it! But would you have asked if he hadn't?" I cried.

"No."

"No!" I stood up and started to walk back down the path, certain for sure that my doubts were plain truth.

"Lovina! Come back here!" I heard.

I kept walking. "Lovina!" he called. Then he came after me and turned me around, holding my elbows. "Look, Lovina, I didn't want to ask you because I don't deserve you. Why, any of the fellows would be glad to marry you and give you a fine home. And I—I don't even have a single silver piece, and won't for some time because I've been consecrated to the temple. These three years I've worked for Brother Joseph without any pay but the keep of my family. I don't know how long it will be till Father gets back from his mission and can take over their care. I didn't think a girl like you would want to marry a fellow with prospects like mine." He looked down at my kid boots, then up at my new palm-leaf bonnet that I couldn't resist buying when I saw it in Miss Ells's shop window. "You've got fine dresses and your father owns property."

"That's the only reason?" I asked, my eyes fastened on his vest button.

"No." Lorin looked towards the water and sighed.

"D-didn't you love me?" There, I'd finally asked!

Lorin groaned and let go of me. Then he admitted, "I tried not to. I tried to forget you, but it didn't work. Even this whole Mississippi River couldn't wash away that love. But you deserve better."

That was enough love for me! I smartly walked Lorin right back to the log, sat him down and placed myself right next to him. He was never getting away from me now! Never! "I'm waiting for the rest—my dearest." My, but my speech was suddenly bold!

When I uttered that endearment, Lorin looked up and took my hand in his. "Do you mean that? Dearest?" he asked earnestly.

I nodded.

Slowly he raised our folded hands to his lips and kissed my fingers. "Do you remember the night when I did that before?" he whispered. His voice was hoarse with emotion.

"Every word and every moment." Through my tears of happiness

I matched his loving glances. "They are each engraved upon my heart forever."

"Mine too. Oh Lovina, are you certain you want to marry an old spider-skinny fellow like me? Ever so many more handsome men have sought your hand. You could marry a man with hair."

"Don't you ever say such a thing again, Lorin Walker! I won't hear of it! To me you are the most handsome man in Nauvoo. I'll soon fatten you up. Already your hair is growing again; and if it doesn't all come back, then every time I look at you I'll remember how I almost lost you through my foolishness, and I'll appreciate you all the more."

That didn't comfort him. He had more concerns. "Say Lovina, you don't just feel sorry for me?"

I rolled my eyes and turned my head. "My goodness, and I thought I had doubts! Why should I feel sorry for you? If you hadn't provoked that man . . ."

Lorin put his hand to his chest and protested, "I provoked that man? What about all the dances you gave him?"

I stood up, mad all over again. "Lorin Walker, you know very well that I did it for the sake of Eliza Partridge! Or didn't she tell you?"

"Sit back down, Lovina. She told me. She told me how you came to her rescue. Besides, maybe Jackson didn't poison me at all."

I sat down and placed my head in my hands.

Lorin put his head in his hands, too. "We can never prove it," he said.

"No, we can't," I agreed.

Dropping his hands, Lorin said, "We'll have to put it behind us and begin our life together. Will you be happy, Lovina? We'll have to live with Brother Joseph."

"Oh." Disappointment filled me because I so looked forward to being mistress of my own little castle. However, Lorin looked so forlorn lest I not marry him on that account that I smiled and said, "Then I won't need so many linens. Perhaps I can be ready this summer."

"This summer? That's four long months away!"

I put my hands up to my teeth and tapped them with my fingers. "Lorin, I must confess that I was not diligent, and my hope chest is but half full. I must make several dresses and things, besides doing chores."

"I hope you're worth the wait."

I looked up quickly to catch the old twinkle in his eye. "Lorin Walker! You are teasing me!"

"Of course I am," he said before he grabbed my hand and kissed it once again.

Log-sitting was proving to be a most dangerous pastime. I thought it a timely moment to abandon the solitude of the log, as the sun was fast lowering on the horizon. So we wandered home, arm in arm, in perfect peace and charity with one another.

Chapter Fourteen

"I couldn't be more happy for you. It was a match ordained by God. To think that I should live to be a great-grandmother!" I was kneeling at the feet of my grandmother, Lucy Mack Smith, to whom I was especially close. I was her eldest grandchild. She was a sweet and fragile woman who wore a lace cap and a black satin dress.

"Grandma Smith! I'm not yet married. You must not even think such things!"

"I'm old enough to think whatever I please without fear of censure. So if I'm looking forward to being a great-grandmother, I'll say it." She began to rock in her polished wooden chair. Drawing away, I said, "I have not yet thought upon such things."

"Well, you'd better start soon. When is the wedding?"

"I must prepare my linens and trousseau and wedding dress, which may take months. My chest is but half full."

She stopped rocking and looked at me. "Spent too much time running about being a belle and not enough time preparing for the one who caught you?"

I was silent. It was all too true. And now I had months of sewing before I could be ready for marriage. "Lorin is willing to wait," I said. What I did not say was that I was, too! I knew how much work husbands and babies were, and I was enjoying my engagement. And perhaps Lorin was enjoying not having a wife to support.

"Well, he won't want to wait forever. You'd better bring me

some of that material to sew a quilt top."

"You'll help me? Oh, Grandma!" I leaned on her lap again.

"Only if you'll occasionally keep me company while I do it."

I rested my head on her lap. "Of course I will."

"He's a fine young man that you've caught yourself."

I looked up at her and smiled. "Oh, I think so too! I love him so much that I imagine all the birds must be singing of it."

"I'm glad to hear it. I must confess that at times I was mightily concerned for you, getting mixed in with that Jackson fellow. Even if he had joined the Church, I didn't much like him."

"Neither did I. And if the truth be told, I'm relieved to be done with him."

At that moment we were interrupted by Aunt Emma, who came into the room like a torrent, with one of her hairpins falling out and her shawl only half about her, mad as a wet cat. Aunt Emma was most often a sweet and calm woman, though strong-willed, so her demeanor startled us.

"Lovina, are you in here?" she called. Upon finding us she said, "You must go home at once! The most dreadful, terrible thing has occurred. Go quickly to your mother—she will need you."

"What is it? Has someone died?"

"Oh, no, nothing like that. Mary will tell you." And placing my pelisse over me, inside out, she shooed me out the door.

I walked out the front gate and crossed the road to the corner. There, coming towards me, was Joseph Jackson, who must have been visiting the Laws once again. In my state of alarm I could hardly behave in a civil manner, and turned and ran quickly across Water Street. (Not that he deserved to be treated with kindness, after his threats to my father and myself and ill treatment to my friends.) So agitated was I that I lifted my petticoats and jumped clear over the fence surrounding our yard! Let it be spread about Nauvoo that I would do even that to avoid Mr. Jackson. That would end the speculation concerning us!

"Yeah for Lovina! Three cheers for Lovina! You're a regular guy!"

Immediately I was surrounded by eighteen to twenty boys—my champions and guardians. "We wouldn't have let 'em steal ya!" shouted one of them. "You were plenty safe—but that was a mighty good jump, skirts and all. What do you say, boys?"

The chant was given out: "Our fathers we'll respect, our mothers we'll protect!" It was the motto of the Boys' Brigade of the Nauvoo Legion.

"Sisters too," my brother John added.

I had the Nauvoo Legion protecting me. "My! No danger shall I fear from henceforth," I said, quoting to them what Shakespeare had once written:

I do not think braver gentlemen,
More active-valiant, or more valiant young,
More daring, or more bold, are now alive,
To grace this latter age with noble deeds.

All the boys lined up at attention and marched proudly around the perimeter of our property.

John confided quietly, "Could be even more dangerous inside, Lovina. There's a whole passel of angry women in the kitchen. I'm steering clear of 'em."

I looked him in the eye. "My conscience is clear. Is yours?"

"Almost."

"Then I'll be the one to enter first." It seemed to me that the worst "crime" the boys had committed was to deprive the Smiths of a lawn that year. All those marching feet tromping it down! And with Mr. Jackson still about, it could go on for months.

Inside I found several of the leading women of Nauvoo, members of the Female Relief Society, assembled about the hearth. Indeed the conversation was heated—no wonder John did not dare to enter! Never had I heard such a babble of voices. Whatever had come to pass?

One sister declared, "I think we should tar and feather him!"

Then Mother said, "In my own mother's day, they would have

settled him with a duel. A mere fifty-dollar fine—pah!" I could not believe Mother would say such a thing.

"I say we try him for murder!" said my mild Aunt Mercy.

"Whatever is the matter?" I asked in great confusion. I was so unprepared for this scene that I did not remove my bonnet. Had Mr. Jackson indeed gotten his promised revenge on Father?

It seemed that he might have done so. Father's character had been murdered and defamed by one Orsimus F. Bostwick; and when Father had immediately taken him to court for slanderous language and won, Bostwick's lawyer, Francis Higbee, said he would take the suit to Carthage. That would spread the lies not only throughout Nauvoo, but about the entire countryside. But the most devastating part of the incident was that he had insulted all of the women of Nauvoo. Bostwick actually claimed that my father, who was the most virtuous man alive, was promiscuous with the widows, and that for half a bushel of meal he himself could gain accommodation with almost any woman in the city. How dared he to say that about the most moral women on the face of the earth! Fie upon him! Once I heard this, I became as righteously indignant as the rest of the sisters! Our virtue had been assailed! Never before had such a thing happened to a whole city of women. We demanded satisfaction.

"The bloodthirsty pimp!"

"Woe to the man who slanders a woman!"

"He and his ilk must be driven from the city!"

"His house should be burned!"

And I added, "He should be left for carrion meat!"

This sort of inflammatory dialogue continued, with sisters coming and going and consuming a crock of jam, until it was past time for suppers to be cooked. Indeed, very few families in Nauvoo ate their meal on time that day, the twenty-sixth of February, 1844.

Nor the next day. Indeed, all women's work was haphazard throughout the city. Orsimus F. Bostwick must have counted himself fortunate to be under protection of the police. Only a healthy respect for the principle of law and order saved Bostwick and Francis Higbee from the angry female population of Nauvoo.

Though fifty dollars was a paltry penance for such a large crime, we were pleased with the prompt action taken by Uncle Joseph in halting the venom of that vile villain. And when Uncle Joseph assigned Brother William Phelps to write a piece on behalf of the sisters for publication in the Neighbor, they channeled their indignation to advising Brother Phelps on the writing of that piece. He became so overwhelmed with offers of assistance that the Relief Society scheduled a meeting for Saturday, to take place in the Assembly Room, for that very purpose. Poor Brother Phelps!

Chapter Fifteen

Though the women of Nauvoo went back to their chores and the city once again followed its course like the river, running clear, clean, and pure and sparkling with righteousness, the heralding of the first steamer of that year—belching, splashing, and squealing its way upriver—brought reminders that the world at large was determined to disturb us from both within and without. The Anti- Mormon Party of Hancock County set aside a day of fasting and prayer for March ninth to pray for the downfall of Uncle Joseph, whom they called "Holy Joe," whereby the pious of all orders were called upon to pray that he might speedily be brought to deep repentance for his blasphemies. They could not tolerate his teachings on the nature of God. Yet on this same "holy" day they planned a supposed "wolf hunt" which in reality was an excuse to pester and mob the Mormons living in outlying areas. It sounded to us as if they were cloaking their desire to enrich themselves with our property under a mantle of piety. Echoes of Missouri!

Father and the brethren met with the temple committee to effect the hastening of the completion of that building before the Saints were forced to leave Nauvoo. For unless Uncle Joseph was elected President, and thereby gained ascendancy over the enemies of the Church, it seemed probable that we would someday, sooner or later, be made to abandon our lovely homes for the Oregon

Territory, where we could at least set up our own government with no one to oppress or afflict us. But before then, we were pledged, every man and woman, to gain our eternal blessings in the temple, God willing. First the building needed finishing—a job that would require several miracles and many dozens of helping hands. As most citizens were vitally concerned about the coming persecutions, thousands were in attendance at a public meeting held outdoors on the temple site on the seventh day of March. It was fine weather for a meeting. Though the meeting started at nine in the morning, when Lorin and I arrived at seven, many of the best benches were already filled. However, we were able to find seats towards the front, Lorin sitting on the men's benches and I right across the aisle on the women's. From there we could see way across the riverbank into Iowa Territory, where the farmers were burning off the prairie preparatory to spring planting. The whole world was a rim of fire and smoke.

"Looks like the end of the world," Lorin said.

"The way the gentiles are behaving in Hancock County, 'tis a wonder it doesn't soon come," said I.

"Not before you marry me, I hope. Though the way you are so slow about sewing . . ."

"Lorin Walker! I'll have you know that I hemmed five sheets this week! And I started on a quilt." I folded my arms primly and would not look at him. When he did not speak, I gave in and turned toward him.

The way Lorin was looking at me made me blush rosily. He was thinking immodest things about the quilt. "We are in a public place," I chided him, then refused to speak to him anymore across the aisle for all to hear.

Many carriages stopped along the edges of the gathering place, and thousands arrived carrying chairs and stools. Soon Lorin was forced with the other men to give his section of seats to the sisters, and I repented of my lost opportunity to plan with him.

Father began the meeting with his favorite topic, the Penny Fund. He called upon the brethren to do as much as the sisters in donating money and said that such a vast multitude could perform a "marvelous work and a wonder," like Isaiah prophesied. In order to do this, we needed to concentrate all of our energies on the building of the temple. Therefore, construction of the Nauvoo House would stop.

Ah! Peace and silence. The Nauvoo House would be a place to house newcomers; and since it was being built directly across the street from our home, I could hear the ringing of the saws and the calls for more bricks. The boys would be disappointed though, for the construction had provided entertainment during otherwise dull days filled with chores.

Uncle Joseph arrived late and went right up to the stand and took over from Father. He commenced to speak about lawyers, referring to the trial of Orsimus F. Bostwick and Francis Higbee's appealing the case to Carthage. There was a great stirring of interest in the sisters' section. Then he referred to some other doings the lawyers had stirred up—just like in the Book of Mormon.

"Amen!" we said.

Father followed Uncle Joseph. He called the lawyers polliwogs, wigglers, and toads, and said they should be ferreted out like rats. My! Father must have been clean fed up with the doings in Nauvoo to speak like that! He was referring to the several anti-Mormon parties spreading rumors about the countryside and creating turmoil within the city. They meant to bring mobs upon Nauvoo by taking such cases as the appeal of Orsimus F. Bostwick to the circuit court in Carthage.

Then Charles Foster, a prominent lawyer in Nauvoo, stood up in the vast crowd and yelled, "Do you mean me?"

The very air held silence at his challenge. Not a petticoat rustle could be heard. Uncle Joseph stood and asked him a question like the Quakers do. "Why did you apply the remarks to yourself?"

"Then I understand you meant me."

"You said it."

Then he threatened Uncle Joseph. So Uncle Joseph, as mayor, fined Brother Charles Foster. Doctor Robert Foster, his brother, stood up to attempt a reconciliation, saying that no one had heard his brother threaten Uncle Joseph. But the thousands all cried out with one voice, "I have!" It seemed that everyone in the city was fed up with amoral lawyers and wrongdoers in our midst.

After the reading of "General Smith's Views of the Powers and Policy of the General Government of the United States," which I had heard at least a dozen times in our home and the Mansion House, they read the draft of Brother Phelps's article entitled, "A Voice of Innocence from Nauvoo." This is what the women were waiting for. Once again not a petticoat rattled, nor a bonnet string stirred.

Brother Phelps referred to the atrocities of Orsimus F. Bostwick as "the blasting breath and poisonous touch of debauchees, vagabonds, and rakes who have jammed themselves into our city to offer strange fire at the shrine of infamy, disgrace, and degradation." Several other quotes and pet phrases that I had heard from the sisters were included in this treatise. Also, "My God! My God! Is there not female virtue and valor enough in this city to let such mean men die of the rot—that the sexton may carry their putrid bodies beyond the limits of the city for food for vultures, eagles, and wolves." That line sounded similar to my suggestion!

He covered everything thoroughly, declaring, "Let the whole virtuous female population of the city, with one voice, declare that the seducer of female chastity, the slanderer of feminine character, or the defamer of the character of the heads of the Church, or the canker worms of our husbands' peace: the prostitutes or their pimps, whether in the character of the elite, lawyer, doctor, or cicisbeo, shall have no place in our houses, in our affections, or in our society."

And so we did declare it again, shouting, "Amen! Amen!"

"Were you satisfied, you bloodthirsty female?" Lorin chafed me on the ride home.

"Quite! It was a masterly understatement."

"Understatement! I never heard the like of it."

"Well, I've heard nothing else for a week. How did you like Charles Foster's face when he asked if the lawyer was himself? A polliwog indeed!"

"Quite a meeting!" He flicked the reins so the horses would speed up.

Feeling justice was satisfied, Nauvoo settled into its normal routine, the women hastening to accomplish their neglected chores. I went to work with a will on the week's washing, grating the clothes up and down the washboard, my hands reddened from the lye soap, all the while wishing I was with Grandma sewing my quilt top. As it was raining, I had to hang the wash before the fire to dry. Yes, we should have washed the day before, but in our excitement we had failed to do so. Today, cleanliness had become a necessity.

I stopped to peer out the window through the raindrops, hoping to catch a glimpse of my love. I often watched for him, hoping he might have a special word or smile for me as he passed by. But he was away working on the temple up the hill—much too far to allow me the pleasure of his occasional company. I had to be satisfied with a few moments of an evening visit with the family. Each night when he called he asked me of my progress on the hope chest, but with all the recent excitement I was unable to reassure him. "Tomorrow I will work hard on my sewing!" I vowed.

And tomorrow I would!

Chapter Sixteen

"Meetings, meetings, meetings! All they ever have is meetings!" Mother complained. Indeed, we never saw Father unless it was to feed him or have family worship, and even then he was so preoccupied with the affairs of the Church and men and things of which he had no right to speak, that he hardly said a word before dashing off to another meeting. "There is such a thing as too many meetings when men cannot even get their corn planted on the farm," Mother said as she cleared the table of dishes.

"Hyrum has hired that done, sister," soothed Aunt Mercy. Indeed, there were many meetings in the month of March. Twice the Female Relief Society met to approve "A Voice of Innocence from Nauvoo." Twice more they planned to meet the next week, for so popular was the meeting that they had to repeat it in order to accommodate all the interested parties. Then Brother King Follett died, necessitating a funeral. Afterward Father's unnamed council met, and met yet again that evening. Many men crowded into the lodge room over Henry Miller's store for that gathering. We retired to our beds with Father still at the meeting.

"Awaken, my family! Awaken!" Father called when he returned and banged a spoon against the pot. "Come and witness the glory of the Lord!"

I jumped out of bed and ran down the stairs with my brothers and sisters.

"What is it, Hyrum?" Mother gasped.

"The sky is alight! It's the Aurora Borealis!"

More practically, Mother said, "Children, wrap yourselves up well or go and put on your warm clothes. Then come out and witness the sight."

Quick as a bunny can hop, I was dressed and down the stairs. Outside, the sky was indeed a glory-filled bowl of lights. Beginning at the north end of the sky, a blue, purple, pink, and yellow river of colors led to the south, with various tributaries branching out to flood all the heavens.

"Papa, is this the end of the world?" little Sarah asked, tugging at his coat.

Father picked her up in his arms. Smiling kindly, he said, "The things we accomplished this night for the kingdom of God are celebrated in heaven."

"Like a party?" she giggled, infected with his joy.

Father laughed. "Yes, Sarah, like a party."

"Like a party at night with lots and lots of candles!" Sarah pronounced. We all laughed.

"Hyrum, what was done at your meeting, if I may ask?" said Mother.

Turning serious, Father told her, "The final foundation stone has at last been laid for this dispensation. The work is done."

Mother began to cry and had to wipe a tear away with her cloak. "And I complained about too many meetings!"

"There have been a great many. But all to the glory of him who made both the heavens and the earth, as we stand here to witness."

As we watched the lights move and change colors, other folks came out of their homes to see the sight—the Markses, the Laws, and the residents of the Mansion House. The Laws stayed close together in their own yard. My brother ran over to join his friends at the Mansion House. Lorin walked over to our home and held my hand in his. His hair was all rumpled up and his shirt was on inside out.

"Is this how you'll look when we are married?" I teased him.

"Will you love me anyway?"

For an answer I moved closer to him and squeezed his hand tightly. "Always," I whispered.

"Even if I lose all my teeth and grow a beard down to my toes and my eyes turn yellow?"

I nodded as I gazed into his eyes.

"You'll be a beautiful bride," he added softly.

"You're supposed to be looking at the party, Lovina and Lorin, not at each other!" Sarah yelled.

My, was I embarrassed! I wanted those colored lights to fall down and cover me! I wanted to run into the house and hide my head under my pillow! But Lorin held onto my hand tightly and said, "Sarah, when you grow up and become a pretty girl like your sister Lovina, you'll have those same lights reflected in your eyes. I can look right into Lovina's eyes and see the party."

"Let me see!" Sarah climbed down from Father's arms. All the family was laughing again. "I don't see any party there."

"That's because I'm the only one who can see it," said Lorin.

Father picked her up in his arms once more and bounced her. "Lorin is right. Someday, someone will see the party in your eyes." He looked at Mother with love.

That next week, other secret meetings were being held in the city. On Sunday night, many people were seen sneaking towards Brother Law's house across the way. Others walked briskly through the wind, attempting to shield their identity from the world with their hats; but as several of those hats blew off, we were aware of who they were. My brother John watched all these proceedings from an upstairs front window and reported them.

One of those men was Joseph Jackson. But as his clothes were always finer than other men's in Nauvoo, he was unable to successfully shield his identity. "They can be up to no good!" I said when I heard John's report. The wind howled through the cracks in the walls. It seemed as if nature was not celebrating that meeting.

Lorin came over that evening and we toasted apples, the last from our winter store, hanging them on strings before the fire. In a small cookpot I stirred a bit of sugar, molasses, and butter to make a candy for them.

"The new Seventies Hall fell down in the wind today." Lorin always had some fresh news to impart. The Seventies Meeting Hall was under construction and hadn't a roof yet.

"All of it?" I asked with surprise.

"Part of the west wall. It'll have to be rebuilt."

"'Tis a shame, with all the effort going for the construction of the temple," said Mother from the corner where she was stitching by the candle.

Lorin said, "That's sure. Say, who are all those people going towards Brother Law's house?"

"John's upstairs keeping count on them. One was our Mr. Jackson," I told him.

"That frontier dandy! I wish he'd leave town!" Lorin said as he slapped his knee and stood up.

I agreed and said, "So do I. I'm half afraid to go out of the house with him lurking about on the streets, talking to people." Pacing in front of the fire as if already part of the family, Lorin said, "The Brigade boys have seen him strutting up and down Main Street passing the time of day with folks. I don't trust that fellow."

"Whatever he's doing with the Laws, nature is testifying against it and is doing her best to call it to a stop. People can hardly gather for their meeting. They are working against the Lord," stated Mother.

The wind blew and howled in its fury, and the snow began to fall.

Chapter Seventeen

The weather stayed angry all that week but cleared again at the weekend. Sunday, the twenty-fourth of March, we were able again to comfortably hold a meeting outdoors at the stand near the temple. Uncle Joseph electrified the audience by revealing the meaning of the secret meetings held at the Laws'. Conspiracy!

As we had been apprised of the revelations beforehand, it was no surprise to our own family. In fact, we were almost persuaded not to attend the meeting, for we had been told that Joseph Jackson had threatened to kill all the Smith family in two weeks! Oh, what dire calamity had I brought upon my family? I laid awake half the night for fear, thinking and thinking. It was all my fault that we were forced to endure this uncertainty and ignominy. How could I bear the shame and degradation of the loss of my reputation before the world? All would point the finger of scorn at me, for I had been the one Mr. Jackson had loved and sought, only to be rejected. It was because of me that he wanted vengeance.

Alas, how was I to know, at the time, the depths of the depravity of his deformed and emaciated character? How was I to know the vicious winds of fortune to which I was exposing us all? Like a skunk that hides its deadly odors under a cloak of soft and attractive fur, he swaggered into town deceiving us all and blasted forth his stench that would forever cling to our garments. Like the serpent, yea, old Satan himself, he went about tempting and whispering false words into the ears of the innocent with his forked tongue! Fie and damnation come down upon him!

Did I not predict that his flattery was false and that he would soon be undone? Would that he were even now utterly undone! Would that this unveiling of his secret plans might banish him from the society of the virtuous forevermore! Oh, that the sacred and noble paths of all the fair cities of the earth might never know the tread of his boot from henceforth and forever! Murderer!

In the small hours of the morning I imagined him crawling up into my window to stab me in my sleep with a large bowie knife. Every creak and whistle of the wind brought me fresh alarm. In the morning, I was glad to see guards upon our porch who were waiting to escort us to the meeting.

But even with the guards in place, I declared, "I cannot go out today!" Besides being fearful of Mr. Jackson, I was very ashamed. To have it made known before the whole city that Mr. Jackson wanted to kill us was more than I might be able to bear. They would surely say that my actions had brought this tribulation upon my family.

"And back down to that bantam cock and his biddy hens? No! Bringing it before the public is the only way to fight him," exclaimed Mother. The image she evoked was ludicrous. Why, he would probably want to hurt us just for thinking such a thing of him!

"Is that what I would be doing by staying home—backing down?" I asked weakly.

"Of course. Now Lovina, God is on our side. Never forget that. Has he not seen us through perils before? Yea, through the fiends of hell itself I walked to visit your father in the jail at Liberty, Missouri, and that while I was sickly and nearly at the gates of death. Should we be afraid of a mere man who is puffed up with his own consequence? Nay. I am not afraid."

Were my terrors of the night silly?

"Remember that we go among friends; friends who love and support you. Remember that."

So with no excuses to give, I went to the meeting. I kept my head concealed as much as possible. Mother sat up so straight and true that I almost thought a poker was stuck up her back.

Uncle Joseph shocked the people of Nauvoo by implicating not only Joseph Jackson, but also Doctor Foster, Chauncey Higbee, and the two Law brothers. He said, "I won't swear out a warrant against them, for I don't fear any of them. They would not scare off an old setting hen." The fear left my heart, and I could even laugh at the picture such imagery brought to my mind. An old stay-at-home setting hen—that was me! Well, I wouldn't scare off!

Then Uncle Joseph said that if he heard any more from the conspirators, he'd publish all the iniquity he knew about them. The congregation was greatly agitated at this. What other iniquities did he know of them? We all wondered. My, did we have a case of scandal itching at our mouths then! It spread like a disease through the crowd. If it hadn't been for the fact that we wanted to hear the next thing Uncle Joseph would say, I'm afraid our tongues would have wagged so hard that they would have fallen out.

But Uncle Joseph changed the tone of the meeting by saying, "If I am guilty, I am willing to bear it." Uncle Joseph always did that. He was the first to acknowledge any fault he had; and when he had an enemy, he was the first to make amends. He taught us that when someone was offended by something we had done, we should examine our every action to see if something we had done inadvertently had given cause for that person to take offense.

Later on in the meeting, Uncle Joseph preached again—this time about truth. He asked, "Have I ever got power unfairly? Did I ever exercise compulsion on any man? Did I not give him the liberty of disbelieving any doctrine I have preached, if he saw fit? Why do not my enemies strike a blow at the doctrine? They cannot do it: it is truth, and I defy all men to upset it. And every tree that bringeth not forth good fruit, God Almighty (and not Joe Smith) shall hew it down and cast it into the fire."

I sat up straighter. That's what the Lord would do to our

enemies—hew them down and cast them into the fire! Fear not, the Lord was on our side! Like David, I was ready to face my own Goliath: Joseph Jackson. I was armed with the stone of truth and the sling of virtue. I lifted my head.

Yet I never got the chance to throw my stone; for Joseph Jackson, craven varmint that he was, slithered out of town with all his fancy dress clothes before the meeting ended.

The Laws, the Fosters, and the Higbees went right home and shut themselves up tight in their houses, even though the day was so pleasant. Old biddy hens! They were scared to death of Uncle Joseph! But Uncle Joseph and Aunt Emma weren't intimidated by them. They went out riding through the town in their carriage. I saw them as they made their way down the street thronged with well- wishers. They returned to find a crowd at their door, anxious for their safety and thirsty for just another drop of information about the "conspiracy." Lorin sauntered over to my house and took me down by the river, where we watched the sun set.

"If you're scared, you could change your name to Walker. That would ensure your safety," Lorin teased.

"Hmm . . . Lovina Walker. How does that sound?"

"Mighty fine. I like it," he said.

Saucily, I said, "Lovina Smith Walker sounds more dignified."

Lorin took my chin in his fingers and looked at me most seriously. "How about 'Dearest,' my love?"

"Oh Lorin, that is best," I whispered.

As we watched the sun set, we followed it in our hearts to the land of perfect bliss and happiness where all true lovers imagine themselves to be travelling—n'er a ripple ever to mar the waters of their future.

The setting sun to light their path across the shining seas,
As they go forth upon the waves, together eternally.

Chapter Eighteen

The next week a veritable tidal wave of relations and sundry friends descended upon our household, come in from the country for April conference. The men crowded into Father's study to confer, while the women attempted to put on a meal of sorts. As it was showering outside, this task was severely hampered by the presence of a great many children underfoot. Both Aunt Lucy and her husband, Arthur Milliken, and Uncle Samuel and Aunt Levira came with their children.

"He took my marbles!" complained Joseph F., my younger brother, pointing at one of the youngsters.

A sling was retrieved. Someone tipped over a bowl of corn meal. It was cleaned up. Another child found a whistle and tried it out. He was sent to the men. Amidst all this confusion, we were overjoyed to be together once more.

"Tell us the news! We've told you our little bit, but with Lovina's engagement and all this rattle tattle I hear about the Smiths being killed off—you must tell!" cried Aunt Lucy and Aunt Levira.

In between settling more childhood altercations, cries for food, and the stirring of the stew and baking of the johnny cakes, the tale was attempted. Then we told of all the doings of the past week.

"Perhaps they really did mean to kill us," worried Aunt Levira.

Aunt Lucy was worried, too. "From what you say of the secret meetings at Brother Law's, I'd say they still have the plan. Just where is this Jackson? Might he come to Colchester and murder me in my sleep?"

I assured her, "Uncle Joseph said he wouldn't scare an old setting hen. He left town, so I've put most of my fears to rest. Mother says to remember the Lord is on our side. He watches over us."

Mother chided, "Martha Ann, now don't squeeze that baby! Lovina, why don't you stop your churning and take the baby up in your arms until the rain stops."

"Doesn't look likely to stop. Could John hold her?"

John looked none too anxious to take on the job. He wiped a hole in the steamy windowpane and looked for the steamboat that was expected.

"I have a new churn that you rock with your feet like a cradle. You put the baby right on top!" Aunt Lucy told us.

Picking up the baby, I said, "To return to the tale, after Uncle Joseph revealed the conspiracy against us, there were at least two meetings held at Brother Law's across the way. Even with guards set all about the street, folks walked right past and went in."

"Whatever are the meetings about?" asked Aunt Lucy.

"Seems that's a secret," Mother answered. "Hyrum claims that it is all a hum, that Jackson spread it around that the Laws wanted to kill the Smiths. He assures me that they have no such plan—that it was all Jackson. But why would they keep on having meetings? And the things that go on! There have been the most peculiar legal maneuverings this past week."

"There was a robbery at the Keystone Store, and they stole five hundred dollars!" I added for good measure.

"And Chauncey Higbee drew a pistol on the police and threatened to shoot! " my brother Joseph F. added.

"Perhaps it would be prudent to continue this conversation after the rain stops," Aunt Mercy suggested, knowing that we could talk more freely without young ears listening.

But Aunt Lucy cried, "Oh! You mustn't! I could not bear to

leave the rest of this tale for later, now that you have tantalized me with a part of it."

Coming away from his window, my brother John spared us the task and explained with great relish. "You see, they had it all planned ahead. This Missourian and two others robbed the store and blamed it on a negro and beat him. The negro came running to Uncle Joseph and told the truth. So the real culprits were arrested and tried. But they found out that the three had previously been tried at a phony trial by Dr. Foster. So he was in on it too. And the robbery took place at the Keystone Store— that's where Jackson had been hanging about. So you see, it was all planned by those desperados. The council couldn't get anything on them, though, because there was no one to testify but a black man. But, despite that, they got those Higbees! That's when Mr. Chauncey Higbee drew a pistol on the marshal and was arrested." He enjoyed having their rapt attention for so long.

I handed John the baby and corrected, "Though he was acquitted on that charge."

"But they got 'em for gambling!" John exclaimed.

"My! It seems a person is not safe in Nauvoo these days," bemoaned Aunt Lucy.

"Uncle Joseph says that there are all sorts of unsavory characters in Nauvoo and that the police should ferret them out," I said, giving the churn a plunge.

"They're all going to be damned and go to where the bad people go," Joseph F. added importantly.

We all stopped and stared at him, shocked. "Now where did you get an idea like that, little Joseph? John, what have you been saying in his presence?" asked Mother, greatly perturbed.

"Nothing, Mama, but the truth! It's only what I hear the men outside of Loomis' hotel say."

"I think it's time to end this conversation. The rain has stopped. You children go outdoors to watch for the steamer. See that you older children watch the young ones. Keep them in the yard." And turning to her guests, Mother continued. "A boatload of immigrants is expected on the St. Croix. Where they'll be housed this weekend, I don't know."

I wanted to finish the tale so I said, "People will make room, Mother. What John omitted to tell you was that the Higbees turned around and arrested the marshal for false imprisonment. They are bound and determined to cause trouble. However, Chauncey Higbee was declared a disorderly person and had to pay all the court costs!"

"And so ends the tale," concluded Aunt Mercy. "I just don't like all these goings-on at all."

"Well, let's hear the good news then, Mary," said Aunt Levira. "When is the wedding?"

The children left the room. Weddings were not as exciting as robberies. I once again bounced the baby. "Lovina has been busy with her hope chest and 'hopes' to be able to be wed this summer," said Mother. "Though she had better get busy on it."

Defending myself, I said, "But I am, I am. There have been so many distractions."

"And we are more. You must have been preparing for our visit for weeks. However, never fear! We are here to help you," promised Aunt Levira.

Aunt Lucy added, "Yes, while our tongues wag, our fingers shall not be idle. Bring on the needles and thread!"

"They're fighting Mama, they're fighting!" little Sarah screamed from outside.

"Lovina, quickly, go and see what it is," said Mother. Returning the baby to Aunt Lucy, I went to see. Indeed, a scuffle was in progress on the wharf. Several boys were ranged against two others, which was grossly unfair. A group of young men who had been watching for the boat and were eager to be the first to spread the news of its arrival surrounded the fight, the arrival of immigrants forgotten. Shouts, threats, and several punches went back and forth.

"Who is fighting?" I called to Sarah.

"It's John and all our cousins against the Laws. They said their pa was going to kill us."

Knowing I could not separate them, I called, "Father! Help!"

Uncle Samuel and Father came running from the office and, immediately perceiving my predicament, headed for the wharf. My own brother John took a swing at another boy, whom I recognized as Richard Law. Richard's only cohort was his brother Thomas, a younger boy, and they were getting the worst of the fight.

"Break it up!" Father said, grabbing cousin Joseph by his shirt collar and brother John by his ear.

Uncle Samuel held the Law boys back.

"Hey, ho, who's having a fight here today?" called Uncle Joseph, who, arm in arm with my Lorin, was on his way to visit his family members.

"He started it," accused Richard Law, pointing to young Joseph. "He called my papa a lily-livered snake hide!"

"And he said his pa would get us all," claimed my brother John. "He's against us and wants to kill us!"

"But he can't, 'cause there are so many Smiths!" added a cousin.

"Nobody is planning to 'get' anyone. And nobody is going to kill all the Smiths," explained Uncle Joseph. He sighed and looked very weary. I wished he could rest and have no burdens. Then he turned to the Law boys, held out his hands, and asked them, "Has anything my sons or nephews said or done caused you offense?"

The two Laws looked down at the ground and dug their shoes into the dirt. Only the Smiths would talk.

"I called his pa a snake," admitted young Joseph.

"I punched first," admitted my brother.

"And I tore off his belt loop," said Joseph F.

My cousin Frederick admitted, "I spanked Thomas's bottom when he couldn't see."

Indeed, it was a trial not to laugh at that last admission.

"And on the other side, was offense given or intended?" Uncle Joseph asked patiently.

Richard Law said as he backed away, "You're not my pa and you can't arrest me 'cause I'm too young. And soon you won't be head of the Church, either."

"Those are strong words," Uncle Joseph said kindly.

"You caused trouble at our mill. But you can't stop us. We done no wrong." And with those words they turned and ran home.

"See what I mean? They won't listen to reason," said John.

"Then let there be a lesson in this: fistfighting does not produce listening ears," said Father.

Chapter Nineteen

During conference I stretched my neck about, almost unscrewing it from its socket, searching the crowd for dear and familiar faces. How had it come to be that there were so many Saints I did not know? Saints from all over Illinois, Iowa, and further away were gathered at the East Grove for conference— such great and vast numbers! Why, I could remember the days when all of the Church could fit within the walls of the Kirtland Temple. Now the work had gone forth to begin to fill the earth. Look how many Saints had gathered to Zion!

Alas, there were Emily and Eliza! But where was Lorin? With his brother and family? I searched and searched until at last I saw them arriving late. Little Mary must have been hard to dress again. Slowly, greeting friends and neighbors, they made their way to the front where we were saving seats for them. Lucy and Olive and the girls came and sat by me. Lorin and the menfolk sat across the aisle. Lorin had a wink for me.

Father was speaking at this session. The night before he had burned up four candles writing his talk. I was proud to see him sitting up there on the stand. He smiled down at all his family who sat together.

At the first session, everyone came in anxious expectation to hear about the fall of William Law and his fellow conspirators, only to be disappointed. Uncle Joseph got right up at the start of the business and told them they weren't going to deal with petty difficulties. Petty difficulties? To me they were not petty. There was a lot of whispering, and we had to be quieted down.

However, Father's talk dealt with these difficulties—that is, after he spoke on the Penny Fund. Father could never open his mouth in public without mentioning the Penny Fund. "The temple must be built!" was his hue and cry. And now it was, "Let's get the roof on this fall!"

Referring to unnamed persons who opposed the work, he compared the apostates to tree toads who climb trees and are continually croaking. Many people smiled at his imagery. It broke the tension we had been under. He said they would hop out of town and not to fear them. He said, "If you hear of anyone in high authority, that he is rather inclined to apostasy, don't let prejudice arise, but pray for him. Never speak reproachfully or disrespectfully; he is in the hands of God."

I glanced over at the Smith boys to watch them squirm with discomfort, remembering the names they had called the Laws. Then I remembered that I, too, had called Joseph Jackson a few choice names—not in public, but I had done it before God. He, too, was in God's hands; and thanks to the Almighty, he had already hopped right out of town. 'Twas a sobering thought how God could bring things to pass.

Father went on to teach us to put down iniquity with good works. "Never undertake to destroy men because they do some evil thing. It is natural for a man to be led, and not driven." I hoped my brothers were listening well.

In the Sunday morning session, I sat by Aunt Emma and Aunt Lucy. Aunt Emma knotted up her handkerchief worrying about Uncle Joseph's talk. Several, like William Law, were croaking that he was a fallen prophet, and others worried that he hadn't published any revelations lately. When conference started, Uncle Joseph had got up and said that by the end of the conference he would prove he was not a fallen prophet. Now, twenty thousand people were waiting for that with expectation. The noise of people visiting was as loud as a steamboat.

"The crowd is so large I just don't know if his lungs will last out," said Aunt Emma. "And there's a storm coming." We could see the clouds rolling across the Iowa prairie towards us.

"The Lord will strengthen his lungs," I assured her, reaching over to still her hand with mine. He had to. So much was at stake with our enemies howling at our gates! I looked at the sky anxiously as I saw people departing for home.

Uncle Joseph arose and told the multitude that if they would remain still and pray in their hearts, the storm would not molest them. Most remained. A hush came over us. And then Uncle Joseph preached his belated funeral sermon for Elder King Follett. No one called him a false prophet after that. Every man, woman, and child in that audience knew for certain that God had spoken through him that day. It seemed that the angels and the Lord himself came down and parted the storm, just like Moses parted the Red Sea. The great thunderclouds rolled in and divided in two. Against them Uncle Joseph's face shone with that whiteness he got when he was inspired from heaven. He taught many glorious things about eternity that none of us had ever heard before or comprehended, and he proved each new idea by the Bible. Each of us was profoundly caught up in what we were witnessing.

He taught that God was once a man as we were! He had a literal body of flesh and bones. As we were His children, we could become Gods ourselves! That thought nigh overpowered me. To become equal with God—was that possible? Yet as I looked at the miracle of the sky, I knew, yes, it was.

Uncle Joseph taught that God had a Father above Him! But He was the God that we worshipped. He said that when the earth was created it was made out of something, not nothing! He held up a ring that was cut to illustrate the principle that if we had a beginning, we would have an end. Since the scriptures taught that we had no end, we could have no beginning.

All about us the storm raged. But we sat breathlessly in the midst of it, the sun shining down upon us as a witness to the testimony of the heavens.

Roll over, sectarian world! That day the truth about God cut through the errors of ages to march forward undaunted, untainted, until it would fill the whole earth. Had I not witnessed it for myself? Had I not witnessed in my short lifetime how in fourteen years the Church had grown to fill this valley? Look upon the masses of the Saints in Zion, twenty thousand strong. Apostates, men, nations, try to stop it! A puny hand could stop the majestic Mississippi before it could stop truth from flowing down upon us and consuming us with its glory. The heavens were on our side.

As this happened, Aunt Emma stopped shredding her handkerchief and the tears rolled down her cheeks. Many hearts were comforted that day as they learned doctrine about loved ones who had passed on to glory and everlasting peace. Uncle Joseph talked about little children who died. He said that they would be given to their mothers to raise again after the resurrection. He and Aunt Emma had lost so many babies that I knew that was what Aunt Emma was crying about. She was filled with hope. How wonderful is the gospel! Sweet is the joy of the truth!

After conference, Aunt Lucy and Aunt Levira stayed on a few more days to help me stitch my quilts. We had two frames set up in the kitchen, and all the family who could be spared worked together. Grandma and Aunt Emma and Lucy Walker had pieced a "Star of David" top for me to quilt, so I was glad of the extra help. Tongues flew as we hashed over all the new doctrines, all the new fashions, and all the old familiar faces we saw.

"Lovina, I must say that I'm agreeably surprised at you this conference," said Aunt Lucy. She was near to my own age and more like a sister or cousin than an aunt. I felt gratified at her compliment and smiled. She continued, "Last conference time, your head was wholly consumed with dances and ball gowns and beaus. I was afraid you'd grown frivolous. Now you've settled down and grown so mature that you make me feel like an old woman."

Everyone laughed at the thought of Aunt Lucy as an old woman. She was the "baby" of the family.

Reaching for more thread, Lucy Walker mused, "I read that Grecian ladies count their ages from the time of their marriages. How old would you be?"

Aunt Lucy giggled. "Much younger than Lovina."

Lorin came to visit and caught the end of the conversation. "This is what I like to see—industry! And all for such a good cause! Sew on, ye armies, sew on!" He clapped his hands together as if to cheer us.

"Perhaps we ought to supply him with a needle," suggested his sister Lucy playfully.

"Alas, I fear my performance would not meet the exacting standards of my fair maiden." Lorin bowed, clowning.

"After those words, shall we dare him?" challenged Aunt Lucy.

All cried, "Yes!" with one voice. And so Lorin plied the needle with the women.

"Perhaps the next lyceum topic will be, 'Shall a man do the work of a woman?'" joked Aunt Mercy.

Lorin replied, "Or, 'Shall a man marry a woman with ten sheets and a new dress or two sheets and an old dress?'"

"What is this, a disagreement, and you're not yet married?" asked Aunt Lucy. She stopped sewing and raised her brows.

I stopped stitching too and watched Lorin. I tapped my foot. I was growing weary of being asked how many sheets I had sewn and when my dresses would be done. They would be done when they were done, and no sooner. I was working as hard as I could! I would need every one of those things. I was not about to marry a poor man like Lorin with nothing at all!

Sometimes you could tell people things before an audience far better than alone. I made the attempt. Looking pointedly at Lorin, I declared, "Lorin forgets that he is taking on responsibility for me and that the more new clothes I bring into our union, the less he himself will have to provide. He is consecrated to the temple." I hoped he would get my message.

"Emma, surely you will see to it that the child has new clothes when necessary," said Aunt Levira.

"Or, should the word be 'wanted?'" returned Lorin. He could say things in public, too!

"Of course the child shall have clothes and all she needs, though I can't promise to spoil her as much as Hyrum does," Aunt Emma said in defense of herself.

Ignoring Aunt Emma, I glared at Lorin. "Are you implying that I have no ability to sacrifice or manage?" I demanded.

"I didn't say anything," Lorin claimed. He looked bewildered.

I got up and left the room, hurt to the quick. How dare he criticize me before my family! Could he not understand? All I was doing was for him! It seemed that I did nothing but sew from morning until nightfall, preparing for our wedding. Did he not notice that? It seemed not. My lip quivered. He did not appreciate me! How could I marry a man who did not hold me in esteem? I turned toward the window and bit my lip, then wiped away a tear or two and sighed. It was hard to be in love.

I waited in my room until Lorin was gone for sure, and not lurking about in the study with the men, before I returned to work on the quilt. I entered the room quietly and took up my needle again. All the pleasure had gone out of my task. Only Aunt Lucy was stitching. She leaned over and confided, "Engagements are such a trial, but he'll get over it. All lovers have a few tiny arguments before they settle in. And you have such a long wait that you can't help but disagree occasionally."

I was not sure at all that I would get over it! My heart was terribly sore and hurting smartly. I jabbed the needle in and out of the design with force. I was not sure at all but that I wanted to wait forever before I married Lorin Walker!

Aunt Lucy continued, "Now, if you had done less gadding about and more sewing last year, you'd be rightly and tightly married by now, with much to look forward to."

Looking up at her, I burst into tears and ran from the room once again. I could not bear the blame!

Chapter Twenty

I found it nigh unto impossible to forgive Lorin for several days, for he had hurt me deeply. Only those we love have the power to inflict a wound so hard to heal. As he forbore to mention linen, dresses, or even wedding dates again, I was able to maintain a degree of composure when in his presence. But all was not well in our particular Zion.

Fortunately, the *Maid of Iowa*, the steamboat owned by members of the Church, was soon expected with a new load of converts! How could one repine with such a prospect? Memories of a certain moonlight cruise the last summer, when we danced to the melodies of the quadrille band, flooded my heart.

Floating across the water, the music had invited us onto the boat. It was my first waltz. Lorin passed me with his partner and stopped and stared. Before, he had treated me much like he treated my younger cousin Julia; but when he saw me dancing with his friends that night, he finally noticed that I was a young lady! When he was able, Lorin partnered me, then walked me about the deck in the moonlight. That began our courtship. Ah, the *Maid of Iowa*! The blessed *Maid of Iowa*!

When the drayman shouted, "Steeeem-bo-at!" doors opened and people flooded the streets repeating the call "Steeeem-bo-at", and more doors opened. Dogs woke up and raced for the river barking to one another, loaded carts were rumbled to the landing, and the boys stopped wrestling in the grass by the Mansion. Uncle

Joseph, wrestling right along with them, ran to the wharf with the boys. Indeed, almost the whole town was on its way.

I stayed behind our fence where it was less crowded and offered a superior view of the proceedings. Mother and Aunt Mercy joined me, anxious to greet the new converts from England, their native land.

What was a puff of smoke beyond the point of the river below the town became a white spot on the water; and by the time the wharf was a mass of anxious greeters, it had become a boat. We could hear chugging and hissing in the distance like the hum of a mosquito, until it grew in magnitude above the cheering of the waiting crowd.

With dreams in their hearts, converts were gathered at the rails gazing at the gleaming white walls of the temple. Soon we on the shore caught the melody of the hymn they sang:

Come all ye sons of Zion,
And let us praise the Lord:
His ransom'd are returning,
According to his word.
In sacred songs, and gladness,
They walk the narrow way,
And thank the Lord who bro't them
To see the latter day.

Some in the crowd met their voices across the waters, every bit as thrilled with the sight of a teeming boatload of zealous hearts singing their way to Zion as those aboard the boat were to be nearing the shores of the city of the Saints. Soon they would meet a prophet of God.

Then gather up for Zion,
Ye saints, throughout the land,
And clear the way before you,
As God shall give command:

Tho' wicked men and devils
Exert their pow'r, 'tis vain,
Since him who is Eternal
Has said you shall obtain.

Touching at last, crowd met crowd and convert met Saint. All met Uncle Joseph. Tears poured down the faces of old friends reunited and folks happy to come home at last. Some were plain glad to be upon solid ground again after months at sea. The crowds gradually dispersed, and each person was absorbed into the city and taken home. Two hundred and ten new residents! Nauvoo was growing fast.

The *Maid of Iowa* slept in her mooring outside my window that night. Lorin slept across the street. I knelt by my window once again, smelling the April blossoms on the air, and thought of them both. Was I wrong to harbor resentment against my love? Was I wrong to try to ease the burden from his shoulders by starting our marriage off with a few nice possessions? A few nice clothes? I remembered all the times our family treasures had been destroyed by mobs—the time they tore Grandma Barden's lace-edged tablecloth and smashed Mother's rocking chair that she had brought from England. It had broken her heart. Was I wicked to desire a few trifles of my very own? Was I wicked to want a home, perhaps after the temple was built and Lorin could start a business? Was I wicked to want a few amenities that my father could provide, like warm quilts for the beds? A wedding dress? A girl needed those things!

What I really needed was some rest, for I had worked hard that day and had not so much as caught a glimpse of Lorin. He had not come to call.

It began to rain.

Preaching the next morning was aboard the Maid of Iowa, under the cover of her deck. Uncle Joseph preached repentance. I hoped that Lorin was listening. I folded my arms and thought how he needed to repent.

Other people needed to repent, too. The church leaders sent one last brother to attempt to reconcile Brother Law to the Church, but he couldn't win him over either. On Thursday, the eighteenth of April, Brother and Sister Law were excommunicated by the council for unchristian conduct. Also excommunicated were William Law's brother, Wilson, and Robert D. Foster. It was a sad day for us all.

When I came home from shopping for lace to sew on the chemise I was making, I found my parents and Aunt Mercy sitting about shedding tears in behalf of their lost souls.

"The neighborhood will never be the same again," sniffled Mother.

"The Church will never be the same again," Father agreed.

"Soon they will leave," added Aunt Mercy with a sigh.

"Jane Law was once a good neighbor," said Mother, nodding.

I told them, "As I walked home, I saw Brother Law going towards the Mansion. He looked as mad as a hailstorm."

"You'd better see what that is all about, Hyrum," said Mother, and immediately Father got up and left to investigate.

Not two hours later, Lorin came to call for me with the carriage waiting outside. "Let's ride out to the north landing," he suggested. I gave my consent, for I was in a mood to have a talk with that particular gentleman.

We rode up Main Street in silence until the houses thinned some, then parked where we could see the river. The landing was empty because no boats were expected. He tied up the reins and dangled the ends in his hands.

"Lovina," he began, "something happened today that made me ponder powerfully."

"Yes, Lorin?" I turned to look at his profile.

"You know Brother Law was excommunicated today. Afterwards he came over to see Brother Joseph with pistols in his hands, determined to 'blow his infernal brains out,' he said."

"Pistols? He had pistols when I saw him?" I felt greatly alarmed at his news.

Lorin turned to me. "Yes. Why? When did you see him?"

"He walked by me on the street on the way to the Mansion."

He dropped the ends of the reins. "Don't you comprehend? You could have been hurt! Life is too precious for us to be estranged from one another. Look at William Law. He's nursed his dissatisfactions until they've festered and infected his soul. Now he's had to be cut off from the Church. Look what it's come to! Pistols!"

"Estranged?" I could hardly speak, for suddenly I felt choked. We were estranged, but it was terrible to hear Lorin say it.

He continued, "I don't want that to happen to us! If we, like William Law, aren't willing to forgive and don't resolve our difficulties, we could stay mad at each other long enough to break it off. Do you want to break off our engagement, Lovina?"

Suddenly I started to cry. Of course I didn't want to end our engagement! It would be worse than the end of the world!

Greatly agitated, running his hands through his hair, Lorin said, "Oh, Lovina, I didn't mean to make you cry. I'd rather break my leg than break our engagement. I just wanted you to see where these feelings we've had are taking us. Don't cry."

I could not stop.

Lorin pulled out his kerchief and wiped my eyes. Holding my chin up so he could look at me, he begged, "Dearest, don't cry. If you want to, I'll talk to Brother Joseph about setting up our own home and you can sew all the quilts and curtains you want. I'll wait. I'll even take on some extra work to purchase a few pots and kettles and boards. Likely your folks and Sister Emma will donate a few accoutrements to the household. What do you say, Lovina?" His generosity only caused me to weep further. "I—I'm fine, Lorin. I j-just love you so." He took my hands in his and I leaned upon his shoulder until my weep was over. At last I was able to look up at him and smile tremulously. "I love you," I whispered again.

"I love you too," he whispered in return. "Let's never disagree again. I cannot bear it."

"I promise." And with that promise in our hearts we turned back to the city of the Saints, with its temple gleaming pink in the sunset. Someday we would enter therein and make more promises.

Chapter Twenty-one

All the blossoms were out on the fruit trees. It was a pleasure to drive to our farm on the prairie and see them. The whole county was a-blossoming.

Were the people in Hancock County as wicked as in the days of Noah? Would the Lord send the floods again? It seemed so, for while the trees were blossoming, the Mississippi River was rising and rising. But the bow had been seen in the sky that year; and Uncle Joseph said that any year the bow was seen, the Lord would not destroy the earth by flood or famine. Well, in the year 1844, he certainly wasn't going to destroy it by drought. Perhaps the crops would flood out and we'd have a famine due to that, but we certainly had no lack of water.

It rained and it rained and it rained. Indeed, it seemed as if the fountains of the deep arose, for the river was higher than in any man's living memory.

Father preached that Enoch had a great soul that swelled wide as eternity. I went home and read about it. The scriptures said that Enoch wept for the iniquity that Mother Earth had to bear upon her crust. I wondered if maybe Enoch was in heaven weeping floods for what the earth had to bear, for iniquity abounded in our county. The *Warsaw Signal* printed malicious lies about the Mormons and stirred up the countryside to hate us and do evil to us. And right here in our own fair city, within the shadow of the temple of God, evil and rebellion stewed. Perhaps those were

Enoch's tears falling! The heart of the Mississippi seemed to swell up with grief. As tears wash away the impurities caught in the eye, the river swelled up to wash away the impurities caught along its banks.

Brother Law's mill, situated along the bank of the river, went under and had to stop its works. Some of the town of Warsaw went under water. Parts of other towns suffered the wrath of Mother Nature also.

Unfortunately, several of Nauvoo's farms suffered from flood and rain as the mighty Mississippi washed away the evil along its banks. Who can stay the hand of the Lord? Who dares to oppose his mighty works? Yea, the waters almost came even to our yard, but by hard work and prayer we were preserved. We built drainage ditches and piled the excess dirt across the way. Not everyone was so fortunate.

The flood of the river brought more converts from England, river travel over the Keokuk rapids being made easier and faster. They too were absorbed into the life of the city.

Several months previous, a certain convert named Thomas A. Lynde had come up the river. What a blessing he proved to be to the city! Mr. Lynde was a tragedian who had played on the stage in New York with the actress Charlotte Cushman. With the help of several others, he got up a theatrical exhibition featuring "Pizzaro or Death of Rollo!" It was the most thrilling thing I ever saw—more so than the Mabie and Howes Circus Company that had come the previous year. Brigham Young took the part of the Peruvian high priest and Porter Rockwell played Davilla. Hiram Clawson and my father's cousin George each had minor parts. The performance just sent shivers up and down my spine!

Lorin took me again the second night, where to my delight I met Emily and Eliza and sat beside them.

"Are you happy in your present situations?" I leaned over and asked them.

"I try to be," confided Emily.

And Eliza said, "I am resigned to my lot and bear all things cheerfully."

Emily, anxious for a crumb of news about the family, begged, "Tell me everything. How is your Grandmother Smith? Did Frederick's tooth come in? Does your Uncle Joseph bear the trials he is under with equanimity? Oh, how I miss them all!"

"Though I know not of Frederick's tooth, I can tell you that Grandmother and Uncle Joseph both appear well. You must ask Lorin, who is with them from day to day."

After looking about the audience to see who else was in attendance, Eliza asked, "When is your wedding?"

"I am not prepared." And with embarrassment I admitted that my sewing was delaying the wedding date.

Emily offered, "You must let us help you. You know how we love to sew."

I clapped my hands together. "Won't Lorin be grateful! Though he is afraid to offend me by telling me so, I know that I am a great trial to him at this time."

Eliza assured me, "I'm certain you are not—see how he looks at you from across the room."

Lorin was talking with Marcellus Bates and smiling my way proudly. We all smiled back at him and nodded.

To return to the subject, Emily asked about the family once more. "How does Brother Joseph bear his trials? I was so terribly concerned when I heard that Charles Foster drew a gun on him while he was performing his duty as mayor of Nauvoo, and that Robert Foster insulted him. Since then he has been in the courtroom with them each day. How does he bear this?"

"He says that his personality is formed so peculiarly as to glory in tribulation," said I. "It keeps him humble."

"That sounds like Brother Joseph!" said Eliza with a smile.

"JOSEPH SMITH FOR PRESIDENT. SIDNEY RIGDON FOR VICE PRESIDENT." Those were the headlines of all the papers in Nauvoo and surrounding towns come May. We all read every word of them avidly. The information ran farther down the columns in papers in other parts of the country; but the Mormons were getting a lot of attention. And more was forthcoming, for hundreds of men had been called out to campaign and incidentally preach the gospel to every state in the Union. Missionaries and wives and families parting from them were everywhere! Each boat took away fathers and husbands and brothers. Each retreating whistle of steam brought on the shedding of the tears of sacrifice. When the last wisp of smoke disappeared over the horizon, families, fatherless, would brace their shoulders and start for home.

Ironically, while families sent away missionaries, Nauvoo had its own particular flood of missionaries. One day Charles Ivins, a former bishop of the Church, came knocking on our door accompanied by his companion, James Blakely. They were missionaries for William Law's reformed church. It seemed that if William Law couldn't have his way over the Lord in the old church, he would start his own. He declared himself its president and prophet. And he was gaining converts! He had collected about two hundred disgruntled and dissatisfied people, and he hoped to oust Uncle Joseph and convert the rest of us!

With much forbearance, Mother invited the two missionaries inside and plied them with johnny cake and milk. They began to teach us what they saw as the truth. With sorrow for our lost and fallen state, they attempted to reclaim us from our evil ways. Mother and Aunt Mercy and Aunty Grinnels listened patiently.

I longed to hit them over the head with a pot! I was busy scouring a nice heavy dutch oven at the time, and my fingers were itching to clap it over their heads! How dare they tell pure and virtuous women such as my mother and aunt to repent! How dare they preach such falsehoods against my uncle and father! But Mother sat quietly and smiled like the fine English lady that she was. She let them say their piece and eat their bellies full until they were thinking rather kindly of the Smiths. Then, without them even knowing it, she taught them that if they believed the revelations given to Joseph Smith prior to 1839, the doctrines taught subsequently were in agreement with them. She said this with patience and love. I put down the scouring, wiped my hands, and listened to her. It was a sight better than their preaching, which had been full of hellfire and damnation! As Mother spoke, I knew her words were true, for glorious burnings filled the room. Could they not feel the power of the spirit? Were they lost to all feeling?

Mother explained afterwards that some men became that way after they had known the truth. They were harder than the gentiles and beyond the power of the spirit.

When I told Lorin about their visit that night, he laughed. Those same two men had called at the Mansion and preached to Uncle Joseph. "Can you picture them teaching the prophet that he is a false prophet?"

"My, they are beyond the power of the spirit," I said with wonderment.

Lorin stopped laughing. "More than that. They seek his blood."

It seemed they truly did, for lawsuit followed lawsuit. Circuit court week was coming again soon, and the "anties" were determined to try Uncle Joseph on as many cases as they could before the circuit judge when he came to Carthage, the Hancock County seat. They had several suits saved up. Uncle Joseph didn't want to be tried in Carthage and attempted to resolve all the difficulties within Nauvoo under the umbrella of the Nauvoo Charter. He knew if they went to Carthage to settle disputes, it would just stir up a mob to do violence against the Saints. That had happened in Missouri. But the "anties" were determined to cause trouble and, with their lawyers, sought to provoke as many incidents as possible to trap and arrest Uncle Joseph.

It was a war of words, a contest of opinions: truth against error, virtue against vice, priesthood against false priesthood, the hosts of heaven against the hosts of hell, the church of God against the dominion of Satan.

It was a purging, a great separation of the righteous from the wicked. Was Joseph Smith a true or a false prophet? Let every man, woman, and child choose for himself. Some households were split, the parents believing one way, the adult children another. Or, like the Ivins family, Charles Ivins going against the Church, the rest choosing to support it. Other families stuck together. But the vast majority chose to follow Uncle Joseph and the Church. No man dared waver or be found wanting, for that was a day of choice.

Chapter Twenty-two

Until I saw it with my own eyes, I would not believe such a thing. But there it was in Lucy Walker's hands, and she was crying. It was the prospectus of the *Nauvoo Expositor*, to be edited by Sylvester Emmonds. He was a young man we had danced with! He had come into Nauvoo a stranger with nothing but the shirt on his back. We had clothed and housed him. How could he turn against us like that? Soon he and the "anties" would be publishing a newspaper against us. The voices of the opposition were growing stronger.

"Lucy, it will come to naught. There is no need to cry over it," I said firmly. "Grandma Smith said it was so."

"I'm not crying over that silly newspaper. I'm crying over my family!" she said, putting the prospectus on her lap so that she could dab at her tears.

For a moment I panicked. "Lorin? Has something happened to Lorin?"

"No, not Lorin," she sniffled. "William and Olive are setting up housekeeping and taking my sisters and brothers with them. I can't go with them." Lucy continued weeping.

I took the paper from her lap so that it would not soil. "It's about time they have their own place. What are you so sad about?"

Lucy wailed, "Olive is to have charge of them. How can she take care of all of them?"

In an attempt to brace her up, I said, "Why, I think it is noble of her to do so, and 'tis only for a time—until your father returns from his mission."

"I can't bear for the family to be separated!" she said through her wet handkerchief.

I tried again to comfort her. "Won't you have Lorin? I have heard no new plan, have you?" I wondered if perhaps we were to live in our own home also. Had Lorin succeeded in asking Uncle Joseph for that boon? Were we also to have our own home? I became greatly excited at the possibility.

"Of course not. You must wait and discuss that with Lorin and Sister Emma. Oh, Lovina, how can I separate from my small ones? They look upon me as their mother."

"Will they be far away?" I asked.

"No."

"Can you not see them daily?"

Lucy lowered her handkerchief. "Yes. But 'tis not at all the same."

I sighed. "I know how you feel," I told her. "I must leave my family for yours. It is at times a most difficult proposition." I thought of how much I treasured them and how I had hesitated to hasten the wedding.

Oddly, that bit of empathy was what dried Lucy's tears. She said, "That is true; you will be leaving them and joining us. To me that will be a comfort indeed. We'll have each other. But I still would wish to go with my brother." And attempting a brave smile she said, "Though I cannot, and must make the best of it."

Later, I inquired of my love what our future was to be. I was still visiting in the Mansion and had spent the afternoon with Grandma.

Lorin took my elbows and faced me with the unfortunate tidings. "Brother Joseph took it to the Lord and was told that for a time we were to remain in his household. My request precipitated the idea that William and Olive were to leave. Do you mind?"

I could not look at Lorin and instead stared at a candlestick on the mantle. All my dreams of a cozy little home of our own crumbled to dust! No curtains. No pots or cupboards or butter churns. No trunks or rocking chairs or brooms. Then I looked out the window at Sarah Rigdon next door, hanging out the laundry, and realized that it also meant—less work.

So smiling gallantly, I drew closer to Lorin and whispered, "Then I have much less sewing to do."

So much did that please him that he drew me down on the settee and began to plan our wedding. He was jubilant. "July! How about the merry, merry month of July?"

Indeed, his enthusiasm affected me. I told him all about my dress and the lace on my new nightcap, and we planned the food for our wedding party.

"Ginger cake. I insist on ginger cake," said Lorin.

"With fruit and cream?"

"I'll say! Lovina, you'll have to sew faster. I'm hungry!"

Many friends were placed on our wedding invitation list. Of course Father would marry us, and all the Smiths and Walkers would be our primary guests. The wedding and the party would take place in our home, and we would spend the first night of our marriage there. My friends would put me to bed, and Lorin's friends would put him to bed. That is why it was so important for me to have lace on my bedclothes. I could not be dowdy for my wedding party! There would be dancing in the main room, and from time to time our friends would come and bring us a treat or two from the table. But for the most part, our party would be ours—Lorin's and mine. Just the two of us.

As we planned, wrote lists, and looked into each other's eyes, I wished with all my heart that our wedding was that very night! Lorin took my hand in his and bestowed kisses on all of my fingertips; and when he looked next at my lips, I thought it prudent to end the conversation and turn it to safer channels. Forbearance made it necessary. He had grown very attractive again. His shoulders were broad and filled his jacket once more.

With regard to Francis M. Higbee, one of the "anties," forbearance was no longer a virtue, so his evil deeds were submitted for publication in the *Neighbor,* lest by his influence some innocents might be led upon the path of iniquity. Mother would not allow me to read the account. I later heard via Lucy that it concerned a disease he had obtained from a "certain French female on the hill" two years previously.

So much had our enemies come out against us that Uncle Joseph thought it necessary to reveal all their iniquities publicly lest any be led astray by their teachings. When on Sunday Uncle Joseph preached about the opposition kingdom set up in defiance of the true kingdom, Father received an anonymous letter calling upon him to make his peace with God, for "HE WOULD SOON DIE." Can our horror be imagined? This was real, written on parchment, not just an idle threat. We could peruse it again and again and wonder from whom it came.

Mother was frightened. I could tell because she kept tugging on her cap, pulling it back and forth. Always it had been Joseph's life in danger, not Hyrum's. Now it was Hyrum—her husband! Aunt Mercy held Mother in her arms to comfort her like a little child. The younger children were not told.

Father took the letter to Uncle Joseph, who concluded that it came from Joseph Jackson and kept it as evidence against him. That was a shock to me. Could Joseph Jackson still want revenge? Still? I marvelled at his pertinacity. Had he not a life to get on with, that he must needs carry his ill feelings with him? What gall of bitterness did he carry in his soul, that he could hate us so? And why? Surely not for unrequited love! After pondering all that day, that night while kneeling to say my prayers, I came to the conclusion that he was a servant of him who fought against the Lord and fell from heaven. Joseph Jackson was one who was in Satan's power, and had come to Nauvoo as his agent. Yes! That was it—the only explanation possible. Why else would he court me so assiduously? Why else would he seek the blood of an innocent father? The very thought of him seeking such revenge was beyond imagination—fantastic. Whoever else but I ever had such a suitor?

Despite this, despite our enemies, and surprising to us all, Uncle Joseph became quite popular as a candidate for President. We read in the *Neighbor* that a St. Louis paper favored him, counting polls taken aboard the steamboats. Overwhelmingly, the vote was for the Mormon leader. Once it was twenty-nine votes for Uncle Joseph, sixteen for Henry Clay, and only seven for Martin Van Buren. The next poll, taken aboard the *Osprey*, was even better with twenty-six for Uncle Joseph, six for Clay, and only two for poor Van Buren.

Uncle Joseph's policies, if adopted by the federal government, would resolve the problems of slavery by buying the slaves from their owners through the sale of public lands. He would reform the system of imprisonment. Texas would be annexed. Many people liked these solutions to our nation's problems. May the seventeenth was the date of the state political convention, and many visitors stepped off the boats onto the landing to lend their support for these policies.

Lorin stopped by for a moment. "The Mansion was full of men, and then they all went over to Brother Joseph's office for the caucus. All those visitors looked puffed up like pouter pigeons, wearing fancy vests with watch fobs and top hats and fancy boots. But in spite of being the center of all the attention, Brother Joseph is in the room upstairs with Sister Emma."

Aunt Emma was feeling poorly. Uncle Joseph could teach all those proud men a thing or two about priorities. Aunt Emma's health was worth ten presidencies to him.

"I hope when we are married you love me that much, dearest," I told Lorin.

"You'd better deserve it," he teased as he tweaked my nose.

"Why, you . . ." I began. But before I could adequately respond, he was gone.

Later that night, there was a barrel of tar burning in front of the Mansion with a huge crowd of men surrounding it. My brothers rushed out to see what would happen. Uncle Joseph came out with his shirtsleeves rolled up and no cravat or coat. He was hoisted up, but instead of being tarred and feathered as I for a moment feared, a band began to play and he was cheered and carried twice around the burning barrel, and then into the Mansion for a celebration.

Chapter Twenty-three

The old homestead had the most exciting vantage point in the whole town. We loved living there. We could see every steamer and all the goods and travelers that landed at the Nauvoo House Wharf and continued up Main Street. The Mansion was within my view as well as the headquarters of the opposition, set up at William Law's. We didn't miss a trick. And now the Nauvoo Legion was to train in front of the Mansion! From my brother's bedroom window I had a view that was the envy of every female in town.

My, they looked magnificent! Row upon row of soldiers paraded in front of our home. There was a veritable forest of them making cuts and thrusts with their bayonets as they marched by. The Nauvoo Legion Band played their horns and drums to keep time. Second came the Calvary. I leaned far out of the window searching for Lorin until I found him. Then I waved my scarf madly. He was much too good a soldier to lift his hand, but knowing I would be at my window he offered a smile in my direction.

Lastly came the Boys' Brigade, with two sturdy youth bearing the painted banner that read, "Our Fathers We'll Respect, Our Mothers We'll Protect." The Brigade looked almost as worthy as Helaman's two thousand stripling warriors! My brother and cousins were among them. I waved my scarf extra hard and gave them a shout—those who had saved me from the clutches of Joseph Jackson. Hurrah! Hurrah!

The visitors to Nauvoo were most impressed with this display of discipline, but William Law was not. His doors and windows remained tightly shut. Just that month he had been court-martialed and removed from his position in the Legion. Such an action must have been a heavy blow to his pride.

Monday, the twentieth of May, he had his pride back, for the circuit court came to Carthage and all the county went as either spectators or testators. Court week was more popular than the circus. All the "anties" went. And every last apostate who had a grudge against Uncle Joseph laid a charge against him. By Tuesday he was in hiding again. Poor Uncle Joseph spent half his life in hiding from frivolous lawsuits got up against him. It was his lot. One minute he was shoveling the ditch to help drain the flood waters, and the next minute he was gone. The man sent to arrest him searched in vain.

Forty Indians came to Nauvoo the next day to counsel with the Big Chief (Uncle Joseph) as they often did. My brother John ran to tell us, and we watched the canoes come down the river and land. Several of them strode up to the Mansion and went in. When they couldn't find Uncle Joseph, they sat on his front lawn to wait. It seemed to me that if Uncle Joseph were to place himself right amongst those Indians, no law officer would dare to take him. They were frightening!

The Indians spent the night in the council room and came to call again at the Mansion the next day. Mother kept the children safely indoors and sent them right upstairs when the red men came across the street and entered our kitchen door, asking for food. They looked solemn as eternity decked in their native pride, with ornaments of feathers, paints, and broaches. They seemed to fill our whole kitchen. Last year one chief had wanted to trade a pony for two of little Martha Ann's golden braids, but Mother wouldn't allow it. She had stood firm before the chief. This year she was taking no chances with a repeat encounter.

Mother passed them some corncake and a string of catfish someone had brought us for our dinner. She smiled politely and spoke kindly. Mother was always a lady. Not knowing what else to do, we bowed to them and they went away.

At three o'clock the cannon was shot off in front of the Mansion for the Indians' entertainment, and a dance was held in the street. I went across and partnered with Lorin. All the Indians sat in a straight line upon their knees like they were praying. I could see my sisters and Joseph F. lined up at the window to watch, so I waved gaily.

"Did little Martha Ann retain her braids?" Lorin asked as he twirled me about.

"Mother put a bonnet on her and won't let her out of the house. The poor child is missing all the fun."

Uncle Joseph came out and stood safe as a house in this crowd. The police stood round the edges of it as an extra precaution. When we were finished dancing, the Indians commenced a dance for us as a gesture of friendship. One man sang strange words using a very few notes, while another man beat out the rhythm with a single drum. The meaning was told to us through an interpreter:

I stood there, I stood there,
The clouds are speaking,
I say, "You are the ruling power,
I do not understand, I only know what I am told,
You are the ruling power, you are now speaking,
This power is yours, O heavens.

They were bearing their testimonies to us! Drums beat and feathers flashed. For two hours we watched them dance, and then the cannon was fired again. After bidding farewell to the Big Chief, they jumped in their canoes and paddled upstream.

Can you wonder that we all loved our fair city and took pride in its consequence along the river? Each new boat brought fresh delight to us, and there were always surprises in store, be they lecturers, statesmen, writers, performers, phrenologists, reporters, politicians, scientists, tourists, converts from all around the world, circuses, or even Indian chiefs. They all found their way to see for themselves the city of the Saints of God and the Nauvoo Temple on the hill.

Although good things came to us, sometimes it was fresh trouble that came our way. This time it was more bad tidings. Our justice of the peace returned from circuit court and said that Foster had been giving false testimony against Uncle Joseph, which was inflaming the mob spirit. So he and Porter Rockwell went the next day and had Foster arrested for perjury.

Father led us in prayer that night, praying, "Father, protect us from thine enemies. Place a hedge between those who are against us and those who are for us. Still the voices of the evil one that rage against thy Saints. Calm the waters in the midst of the storm, and keep us safe in thine hand. Be with those who lead us, that we might hold our tongues and speak only words of wisdom," he prayed. Much more did he say as we knelt together, but those words stuck right in my mind, troubled as I was with the constant reports we heard from Court Week in Carthage.

Friday I ran over to the Red Brick Store to procure another three inches of the lace I needed to sew on my corset cover. Mr. Bidamon sold it to me for plain cash. Uncle Joseph had hired him to run the business and he wouldn't accept credit, even mine. An elderly sister wearing a large black flowered bonnet, who I did not recognize but who apparently recognized me as the daughter of Hyrum Smith, chided me, "Can't think as to how you got yourself romantic with a no-good scoundrel like that Jackson! Ought to watch out for yourself, you should!" She shook her black gloved finger at me briskly.

I did not know how to reply to her without either revealing our secret or sounding mighty rude! I held my tongue with great difficulty and turned away from her. Joseph Jackson was in Carthage, and all of Nauvoo was talking about the ruckus he was creating there. It seemed he was indeed determined to have his revenge upon the Smiths! Uncle Joseph was once again in hiding.

The next day the news was brought that only two charges were brought against Uncle Joseph. All the rest were thrown out of court. They said that Francis Higbee swore so hard while bringing forth his suit against Uncle Joseph that his testimony was rejected. I believed his character was given over to the father of lies.

Joseph Jackson's charge that Uncle Joseph committed perjury held. Oh, Mr. Jackson was a sly one! He was not only sly, but intelligent, educated, and talented. Indeed, his talents made him a formidable enemy. When evening came, it was rumored that he was in Nauvoo. I felt frightened. The very idea of coming face to face with that man made my toes curl.

"Be not afeared," said Lorin. "The officers are after him for threatening life." Nevertheless, Lorin was careful to remain with me until Father returned home. I was able to ply him with quite a large amount of food. I was having great success at fattening him up. He looked much the old Lorin of Christmas days, minus just a few strands of hair. But that gave increased consequence to his brow. I thought him the most handsome man of my acquaintance and told him so, which pleased him greatly.

Sunday, Uncle Joseph preached from the stand and related the whole history of the trial of a Mr. Simpson. That was the trial during which Jackson was claiming Uncle Joseph had committed perjury. Uncle Joseph said to us, preaching against Jackson, "He has committed murder, robbery, and perjury; and I can prove it by half a dozen witnesses. During the trial of Mr. Simpson, Jackson got up and said of me, 'By God, he is innocent,' and now swears that I am guilty of perjury. Also, Jackson threatened my life." Uncle Joseph said he could prove that he was innocent of any charge brought against him, because for the past three years clerks had followed him about and recorded every deed he did. No one could prove anything against him. Then he admonished us to bear all things. "Be meek and lowly, upright and pure; render good for evil." He said that we shall triumph and hold the Church together, but if we bear these things, "we shall then triumph more gloriously."

I took that advice much to heart, for the more notorious Jackson became, the more my former association with him was discussed. Though my acquaintance with him had been very brief, the story grew with each telling until I occasionally overheard whispers against my character from folks who did not know me well. The black-hatted sister was not the only one to think wrongly of me. "She attracted Jackson and allowed him to talk love to her," they said. Though their words wounded me deeply and I had cause to avoid public places, I knew better. I had done no wrong. And my friends knew better than to believe such a thing of me. God knew the truth. And like Uncle Joseph said, the truth would triumph in time.

Lorin felt all these things deeply in my behalf, but I counseled him to do as Uncle Joseph said, to render good for evil, that we might triumph more gloriously. We were bound to triumph because truth was on our side, so why not do so with glory? One could not blame the people; they did not know my circumstances and could never know, as it was not my tale to tell. I could not blame them. Had I not lived it, I too would have thought the same.

Chapter Twenty-four

The second week of circuit court, Uncle Joseph decided to face the charges and the mobs outright. "Must you go, Hyrum?" Mother queried the next day as Father prepared to accompany Uncle Joseph to Carthage. Mother had asked that question several times already; and though she put on a brave front, I knew she was thinking of the threatening note that had come a few weeks before, for her eyelid twitched as she ironed Father's cravat.

Father put her iron back on the fire and took her hands in his. "Mary, I am not on trial. But if I did not accompany Joseph, I could never face him again. I could never face the Lord or my father when I leave this earth. Joseph is my brother. I know there is danger, but I must do the right thing. If I do, only then do I have the promise of the Lord's protection. My place is beside Joseph."

"I—I understand," she answered.

Then Father took her in his arms and said his goodbyes. He took all of us in his arms and kissed us one last time. "I'll be back by nightfall or in a few days at worst. God bless you all." And giving Mother one last caress, he was gone.

Mother sat like a stone in the chair by the fireplace. I knew she was remembering the time Father was carried away to jail in Missouri with Uncle Joseph. At that time she had been recovering from sickness. Her sorrow had kept her down for many months. If it hadn't been for Aunt Mercy and Aunty Grinnels, we might all have perished.

Aunt Mercy understood Mother's fears and let her just sit for a while, staring at the wall. I felt responsible; it was partly through me that Father was in danger. I tried to work extra hard to make up for it, for I could not vindicate myself before them. Not once had Mother accused me of bringing the trouble upon them, but I felt dreadful. Joseph Jackson was in Carthage waiting for Father with his pistols. He could shoot him! Would Father come back? Would the Lord protect him?

"I think we should offer another prayer," Aunt Mercy suggested.

She gathered all the children, and we knelt down together. Some of the fear was removed from us as we sang:

Let thy kingdom, blessed Savior,
Come and bid our troubles cease;
Come, oh come! and reign forever,
God of love and prince of peace;
Visit now poor bleeding Zion,
Hear thy people mourn and weep;
Day and night thy lambs are crying,
Come, good Shepherd, feed thy sheep.
Come, good Lord, with courage arm us,
Persecution rages here—
Nothing, Lord, we know can harm us,
While our Shepherd is so near.
Glory, glory, be to Jesus,
At his name our hearts do leap;
He both comforts us and frees us,
The good shepherd feeds his sheep.

Blinking back her tears, Mother rose and waved her hands about as if they needed to keep busy to forget, saying, "All this worrying won't do the work. Up and about! Lovina, see to the washing. John, see to the wood. You two little girls see to the candle dipping. I'm going to make soap. That will keep my mind busy!" It was good to see Mother strong again.

"Aw, Mama, I wanted to go fishing!" said John.

"After you chop the wood."

My hands were red and crinkled by the time I had all the wash hanging on the line. Not much was happening that day with so many of the brethren off on missions and many more gone off to Carthage with the church leaders. Lorin's brother William went along with them, but Lorin stayed behind. Aunt Emma was sick again.

"Lovina! Lovina!"

I looked up to see my two friends, Eliza and Emily Partridge, tripping down Main Street. Oh, happy day! Ecstatically we greeted one another. I showed them my chapped hands.

"Try bear grease. 'Tis not elegant, but nothing works better," suggested Eliza.

Emily advised, "That elegant Creme de Salitol they sell at Haven's Drug up on the hill does not work nearly so well."

"What brings you?" called Mother. She was forming soap balls while sitting outside on the bench between the well and her fire.

Walking over to Mother, Eliza said, "We came to express our concern."

"Oh, Lovina, we feel we are to blame for Brother Hyrum's danger!" cried Emily, taking my hands in hers.

I begged her, "You mustn't! You mustn't feel that way! The blame is all mine. Our plan went all awry."

Overhearing us, Mother asked Eliza, "What blame? What danger? What plan are they speaking of?"

Eliza turned to Emily.

Walking over to Mother, Emily confessed for the three of us, "All the town is speaking of the torments that were brought upon your family by Joseph Jackson and his association with Lovina. We felt it incumbent on ourselves to take the blame."

Mother became very serious and put down her basket of soap balls. "What blame do you deserve?"

Emily began, "Last January, when we were to be sent away and Brother Hyrum intervened . . ."

Eliza then cautioned Emily to hold her tongue as she spoke.

Emily continued, "You were aware of the circumstances, Sister Smith. But what we didn't reveal was that it would not have been possible for us to remain in Nauvoo if it had not been for the generosity of your daughter in luring away Mr. Jackson from Eliza. He was hanging after her. It would not do. I urged Lovina to serve as a decoy."

"Did you do this, Lovina?"

"Yes. I lured away Mr. Jackson. I'm so sorry, Mother." I admitted this freely, thus lightening my burden of guilt.

"You must not blame her! She did it for our sakes and we did not expect it to be a large undertaking," Eliza implored my mother lest she punish me for my transgression.

"We feel we must reveal our part to the world and save her from ruin," said Emily. "It's not fair for her to endure the censure of the world."

"The less said the wiser," said Aunt Mercy, who had joined us.

We all waited for Mother to speak, anxiously watching every expression cross her face. Finally she said sensibly, "No one is going to ruin Lovina. She is happily engaged to as fine a young man as can be found. People should keep their tongues to themselves. Mercy is right and her counsel wisdom."

Emily groaned, "I was afraid you would say that."

But Eliza said with a sigh, "They are right, Emily. Lovina must continue to bear our censure."

Mother said, "When Lovina stepped into the breach, your course appeared best. One event led to another and could not be foreseen. We must not berate ourselves or each other, for the blame lies at the door of human weakness. Not one of us is perfect yet. Now may the grace of Christ cover our weakness. Though it cannot be told now, Lovina has displayed a most extraordinary degree of friendship. For that I am proud. She'll have to see her promise through."

I added for good measure, "None of us knew the sort of man we were dealing with! He appeared amiable and was in our company. I truly believe he was sent to us by the devil himself!"

Eliza appeared much taken with this thought, as if that explanation had never occurred to her. "Lovina, you may be right!"

I assured her, "He did not love either of us, but came here on purpose to stir up trouble. That I believe."

Eliza said, "I see it now. Yes, you are right. He asked several highly impertinent questions of me . . ."

"Once he asked me where I slept!" said Emily.

"It is all in character, now that we know worse of him," said Mother. "My advice is for us to put the matter from our minds and leave it to God." She once again took up her soap balls.

Aunt Mercy and I went to the Mansion to be with Aunt Emma during the evening. She was ill, and was not bearing Uncle Joseph's absence well. Several times she was sick and had to be tended to.

"What if Joseph does not return?" she whispered, turning a wan countenance to us. "Once Joseph Jackson came to my door and boasted that he was the wickedest man in the world. His words have been proven true. Now he wishes to kill my husband." I nearly dropped the bowl I was carrying! Joseph Jackson the wickedest man in the world! And I had danced with him? The wickedest man in the world wanted to marry me? I could scarcely take it in. Such a sickness came over me at the thought that I nearly had recourse to use that bowl also.

Aunt Mercy answered Emma as she wiped her brow with a cold, wet rag, "Now, dear, we must have faith in the Almighty. The children have been praying, and you know Brother Joseph says when the children pray he'll be safe."

"I know," Aunt Emma sighed.

At dusk Lorin sighted Uncle Joseph, Father, his brother William, and others riding down the road and called out to us. Rising right up from her bed of affliction, Aunt Emma hurried down the stairs and to the door of the house. "Joseph! Joseph!", she cried with relief.

His horse, Old Charley, pranced home, the proudest animal alive, for he was bearing the Prophet of the Lord. Uncle Joseph alighted and embraced his wife and children. Safe again! Crowds gathered to the Mansion to hear the news. Aunt Emma clung to Uncle Joseph's arm.

No, there was no trial. They found Judge Thomas to be the perfect gentleman, but the case was deferred to the next court session. Yes, they were unmolested. Yes, Higbee was there, but Porter struck him down. At this a cheer went up, for Higbee deserved it and Porter Rockwell was not one to bear insults well. No, the Fosters were quite amiable this time. Yes, Jackson was there and threatened us. No, we did not arrest him. We left the skunk behind to stink up Carthage. We mean no harm to any man. "I will triumph every time!" said Uncle Joseph, whereupon cheers were given. "We have enemies about us who thirst for our blood. Let them come! I'll come out on top every time! None can stay the hand of the Lord."

How glad we were to have Father and Uncle Joseph home safely! Our prayers were answered. The children hung about Father's legs all the way home.

And myself, I was mercifully glad I was to be rid of Jackson at last. He had not succeeded. A whole debt load of guilt was lifted from me. He could do us no harm now—the polliwog!

Chapter Twenty-five

That was not the last kick of the frog. Failing to gain his vengeance at the circuit court, on the first of June Mr. Jackson struck again—this time through the press. He published an article in the *Warsaw Signal* entitled "Startling Disclosures," which he asserted was a "statement of facts." How dared he to make that claim before heaven or hell? It was the grossest outrage perpetrated by the pen or press! Facts, indeed! He actually maintained that he had been in Uncle Joseph's confidence and had been hired by him as an assassin. Assassin? How dared he to make such a statement? His audacity went beyond all bounds. The man was mad. He called the police a "ruffian band" and said that the leaders of the Church were counterfeiting money. Well, someone was, but not the Church.

An ordinance was passed by the city council not to allow any paper money at all to be used. Upon investigation, it was found that the "bogus" being passed around the countryside was actually being issued by Joseph Jackson himself, along with William Law and the "anties." So that was his business! I had wondered why a wanderer had so much money to spare for fancy gentleman's clothes! He probably could not remain long in one place lest he be found out. My, the tongues wagged over that news!

Now when we shopped at a store, if we had not silver or gold, we carried a chicken or eggs or a pound of cheese in our bag. It grew quite humorous at times to watch the trading. One shopkeeper could not take another chicken, for he had too many in his coop; so the buyer took off her bonnet and traded that for a pound of sugar. Another brother traded his shirt for a garden tool and walked home with a blanket around him.

One thing came of "Startling Disclosures"—my own justification. For in the article Joseph Jackson revealed himself to have been sent to Nauvoo by none less than Sheriff Harmon T. Wilson himself, sheriff of Carthage and avowed enemy to the Mormons. Joseph Jackson proclaimed himself a spy!

Now all and sundry knew he was not, nor had ever been, in love with me! Now all knew that I had not sought his affections! I was vindicated. Hah! Truth had triumphed—gloriously! Little did Joseph Jackson know the favor he was doing me by writing his wicked article. Little did he know what joy he brought to my heart. Now I might walk the streets of Nauvoo with impunity, not feeling that every eye followed me.

However justified was my own moral character, the women of Nauvoo were once again to be maligned in total. For on the seventh day of June in the year 1844, the first and only issue of the *Nauvoo Expositor* was published. A more blasphemous and libelous piece was never issued in any town in America. It even topped Jackson's "Startling Disclosures."

Piqued at their expulsion from the Church, the "anties" actually compared our church courts to the medieval Catholic Inquisition. Imagine! After all those brethren had been sent to reconcile them to the Church, they could say that?

They claimed we were being led into paths of vice and debauchery through the theatre. I myself thought that opinion extremely unenlightened. They also argued that we were combining church and state since Uncle Joseph was in politics. It seemed that they thought it well to have a president who was not religious, rather than have one who feared God.

But their chief argument was against the doctrines taught in Uncle Joseph's funeral sermon for Elder King Follett. We knew they were not blasphemous, for had the heavens not parted? Had not every doctrine been proved from the Bible itself?

All these criticisms and opinions we could tolerate, but when we read, "Our hearts have mourned and bled at the wretched and miserable condition of females in this place," and, "It is difficult—perhaps impossible to describe the wretchedness of females in this place, without wounding the feelings of the benevolent, or shocking the delicacy of the refined . . .", we were sorely and grievously affronted. We sisters considered ourselves enlightened and emancipated from the bonds of error and darkness. The gospel taught that women were the equals of men— partners. Truth had come at last. Uncle Joseph taught that he who would lead, must do so by serving. Did not he himself, as head of the house, lead in such a way that he was willing to perform the most menial task for Aunt Emma? Had I not seen him countless times doing so—sweeping, cooking, nursing, borrowing flour, and changing a child's clothing? Just try to find a gentile who would do such things! Uncle Joseph taught that in heaven women would have a choice: if their husbands were not kind to them on earth, they could be given to another more worthy of them. That was justice! Search the whole earth for such a teaching, and would you find it? Nay. Only in Nauvoo.

Furthermore, once again our virtue had been assailed—this time much more publicly. Rise up, ye women of Zion! If Orsimus F. Bostwick had been hated, how much more so Sylvester Emmonds and his mad cronies! Throughout the length and breadth of the city the cry went forth: To arms! Women unite! Blast this filth from the face of the land!

However, Uncle Joseph calmed us. He assured one and all that the problem would be taken care of by due process of law. He talked to all of us in groups until he was hoarse.

We waited, and waited, and waited three long days for the deliberations of the city council to cease, ready to take matters into our own hands if the men did not resolve the problem. We were determined that it not happen again. During this process, several brethren were called to testify, and they revealed all sorts of mischief that Jackson and the Laws had been engaged in.

It came out that William Law had offered Jackson five hundred dollars to kill Father. They told about Jackson's bogus making business, and about his threat to abduct me. Father even said that William Law had confessed to him that he was an adulterer! Oh, my! A brother testified that Joseph Jackson had given him stolen jewelry as surety for money he borrowed from him, and had urged him to go into business making bogus with him. When he refused, Jackson threatened his life if he told of it. Another brother said that Jackson had told him he desired to be a highway robber. Much else was brought forth at this time, and as the evidence grew, so did our determination to rid the city of the *Expositor*.

Meanwhile, someone set fire to Sister Law's laundry hanging on the line. We could see the flames leaping into the air. Jane Law tried to put it out with water from the well. Fortunately, the line was isolated from the house and outbuildings; otherwise, it could have been very serious. The culprit who started the fire was never apprehended, and not one person minded. It seemed fitting.

"Do you know anything about this?" Father questioned John. He stood up tall and straight and said, "No, sir. I think it was one of the sisters who did it."

After three days the city marshal, John P. Greene, along with several men, put an end to the *Expositor* in an orderly and proper and law-abiding manner. They carried the press out into the street and broke it, then pied the type and burned all the papers they could find.

Such a celebration there was in every home in Zion! We had suet pudding for dinner that night.

The Laws, the Fosters, and the Higbees packed right up and left town for good. All the other "anties" put their property up for sale. Good riddance to them! They and their insinuations were no longer to be tolerated.

Of course they ran to Carthage and the ruffians with their tittle-tattles and lies about mobs destroying their precious paper. Hah! Would that they had let the sisters do that very thing! But no, we sat at home with our sewing and cooking and laundry, calmly and matter-of-factly waiting to be vindicated. Was there a mob? No! A thousand times no!

At last the apostates had something substantial and concrete against the leaders of the Church that might hold up in court. For the past several months, petty lawsuits had flown back and forth in an attempt to drag Uncle Joseph to trial in the "mob capital," as we called Carthage, where the Nauvoo City Charter would offer him no protection. Over and over we had remained calm and offered no provocation. But now they had something controversial on us. The city had destroyed the press. "Freedom of the press was denied! Illegal!" they cried, forgetting that it was a common legal procedure to destroy such nuisances. There was legal precedent in our state for such an occurrence. Not to mention that in Jackson County, Missouri, our press had been destroyed and nobody had been tried for it! And that paper had not been a nuisance.

A mass meeting of citizens was held in Carthage the next day. We read in the *Warsaw Signal*: "RESOLVED that we hold ourselves at all times in readiness to co-operate with our fellow-citizens in this State to utterly exterminate the wicked and abominable Mormon leaders, the authors of our troubles. RESOLVED that the adherents of Smith, as a body, should be driven from the surrounding settlements, into Nauvoo. That the Prophet and his miscreant adherents, should then be demanded at their hands, and if not surrendered, a war of extermination should be waged, to their entire destruction if necessary for our protection, of his adherents." It could have been written by our old enemy, Governor Boggs himself.

When we read that, Lorin held me against his shoulder as I cried. I felt frightened. What if once again we were under an extermination order? And so many of the brethren were gone from Nauvoo to campaign!

"They must be doing some powerful preaching to shake up the kingdom of the devil this much," Lorin reasoned.

"Do you think so?" I lifted my tear-stained cheeks and looked into his eyes.

"Certainly. Why else would they gnash their teeth so?"

"Oh, Lorin!" I sobbed.

"Nobody is going to hurt you. You forget that the Nauvoo Legion is the grandest force in the West. No other force is so large or disciplined. Even with the elders gone to preach, we have more men than any other army. Why, they're scared to death of us!"

Lorin would certainly know. He was in charge of arming the men. He knew exactly how strong we were. I placed my trust in his confidence.

The first blow of mob power fell on the twelfth of June. Constable Bettisworth of Carthage came to Nauvoo with a warrant to arrest the whole city council for committing a riot. Imagine that! He wanted them to come with him to Carthage to be tried before a justice of the peace. However, Uncle Joseph gave himself and the city council up to be tried right in Nauvoo. We had our own proper justice of the peace. They were soon discharged.

The second and much more cruel blow fell on Saturday the fifteenth. Hundreds of refugees poured into Nauvoo, bereft of homes and possessions at the hands of the mob. One family had their barn burned, another lost everything they owned. The stories they told made the blood run cold in our veins. Men came with blackened faces to do their terrible deeds at the behest of the notorious Colonel Levi Williams. He was a drunkard who had come into importance when people started persecuting the Mormons. It was his road to glory. EXTERMINATION! DRIVE THE MORMONS FROM THE STATE! How those words rang familiarly in our ears. The exiles were taken in and comforted.

Posthaste, affidavits and letters were sent to Governor Ford of the state of Illinois to intervene in the conflict. It was hoped that he was a patriot.

Sunday the sixteenth, we went to hear Uncle Joseph preach at the stand. All in the crowd were concerned about the attacks and looked to Uncle Joseph for guidance, like sheep look to their shepherd. Our hearts beat as one. He said that the Church was being purged, that he was not a false prophet and he proceeded to prove it by the Bible.

I knew he was not a false prophet and I was determined to stand firm, though I be driven across the raging river. William Law had prophesied that Uncle Joseph would never preach again. Well, he was preaching. Like Christ, he was persecuted for blasphemy, for declaring many Gods. Christ had declared himself the Son of God. Uncle Joseph was but his prophet. He had always taught that there were three separate Gods in the Godhead, not one. And now the apostates thought him wrong to teach this thing that they had accepted before.

It began to rain, and still Uncle Joseph preached. Many people ran for cover. I did not hear all of his sermon.

Later the brethren met again and Lorin went. They were told to make no disturbance and to prepare their arms. A group was selected to act as emissaries to the surrounding towns to allay the mob spirit.

Would it? Could the hand of the devil be stayed? So much evil was reported against us that I doubted it. But let it not be said that we would die without an attempt to allay the mob spirit! The flood waters rose again.

Chapter Twenty-six

I didn't see Lorin after that, for he was desperately busy preparing the arms for the Nauvoo Legion under the direction of Brother Turley, a gunsmith. They worked through Sunday night and Monday, insuring that all was in readiness for an attack from the mob.

In the morning I received a note from Lorin. "My Dearest," it said, "Please add to the burden of your sewing." Sewing? Who could care about sewing a wedding dress at such a time? However, I read on: "My uniform is in a dreadful state and I need it tomorrow. Do you see how desperately I need a wife?" Well, he almost had one—me! I was tickled to serve him in that capacity; and despite our danger, I wore a smile as large as sunshine.

I crossed the road to the Mansion and went inside. What a busy hive of men—signing papers, rushing off to collect supplies or to find a certain individual. And in the center of the storm of activity, Uncle Joseph sat behind his desk, his hair all askew as if he had not had a bit of sleep.

I saw Jane Manning coming from the kitchen and called, "Jane! I must prepare Lorin's uniform. Can you get it for me?"

We all loved Jane, a negro convert who had walked a thousand miles barefoot to see a prophet of God after her baptism. She was freeborn and worked for Uncle Joseph.

Jane shook her black curls and declared, "We-ll, ain't that fittin'! Takin' care o' yore man. When's the weddin'?"

"July."

"If I was yo, I'd be a might bit hasty. These times is bad. Yo never knows."

As I sewed, I thought of Jane's words. One never did know. The order had gone to the printer for invitations to a wedding in July. Aunty Grinnels was preparing candy and jams for a jelly roll, working out in the summer kitchen. I was nearly prepared. My dress was half done, and my trunk was filled with beautifully embroidered sheets and three quilts. I was the proud owner of two goose down pillows and a lace table runner. And my trousseau was complete. Could we move the wedding ahead? Should we? With these troublous times, it would be a great comfort indeed to be safely married.

Such a joy it was to do this small service for Lorin! His uniform smelt of soil and horse and gunpowder. When I was done cleaning it, it smelled of soap and fresh air. As I resewed every button securely, I thought lovingly how the jacket would fit over his wide shoulders. I thought braid would add to their consequence, so added that along the seam. I pressed his pants until they were stiff and put a spit on his boots until I could fairly see my own reflection in them. I felt almost wifely—or at least like a little girl playing house.

Lorin would be the finest-looking soldier in the Legion, although I was certain that all over the city other sisters were thinking the same thing about their men. And I was one of them! I was part of the great army behind the army. How proud I was to serve in some small way. All the city was toiling, and at the landing large numbers of people arrived and departed on crowded boats. We went outside to lean over our fence, hoping to catch a bit of the news. Many families were frightened by the threats of the mob and packed up and left the city for St. Louis or Cincinnati; others came to Nauvoo for protection, bringing stories of burnings and more mobs gathering. It was reported that steamboats full of Missourians were coming across to Warsaw. Others came into town to report that the Laws planned to burn the

Nauvoo Neighbor printing office in retaliation for the destruction of the *Expositor* press. Someone even claimed a warship was coming up the river to land at Nauvoo! That struck fear into my heart! How could we fight a warship? We had no Navy. A cannon was placed on the wharf.

Mother said that we should continue our labors, trust in the Lord, and do our part. Father retired to his study to write letters calling the twelve apostles home at this time of emergency. That evening we got the true word. Shadrach Roundy and Stephen Markham had gone scouting in the vicinity of Warsaw and Carthage, confirming our fears that mobs were indeed assembling with threats of immediate attack. They found no proof for the tale of the warship. But they learned that the mobs certainly intended to exterminate the Mormons!!

Word spread fast. Few slept that night, and guards were put on duty throughout the city. Though there were many armed men about the landing and near our house and the Mansion, every few minutes I arose and checked the river view from my window. I was still afraid of the warship. Towards morning, I grew so weary that at last I slept for a time.

Before dawn, Lorin called for his uniform; and owing to my lack of sleep, he witnessed me in my robe and bedclothes. But what did that matter at such a perilous time?

In the darkness he slipped me a revolver. "Just in case," he whispered. "I'll work better knowing you have this. Don't use it unless you must, but here by the water you are in danger."

I hefted the thing in my hands. It was tiny enough to fit into a large skirt pocket.

"Can you shoot?" Lorin asked me.

"I've done so, but I'm not always accurate."

"That's not important. The sight of a madwoman with a gun would frighten any man away."

"Lorin!"

"You're not a madwoman! I only meant—oh, I'm so weary that I don't know what I meant."

"I'm tired, too."

Lorin held out his arms for comfort and I went right into them. I wanted never to leave them.

"Can we be married soon?" I whispered into his shirt.

"What about your dress?" Lorin asked against my hair.

"I don't care about my dress. I only want you."

He held me back for a moment, greatly surprised. "Lovina! All these months, you've talked about nothing but that dress! What about the wedding party? And the invitations?"

I was so tired that I began to cry. "Who cares? I only want to stay forevermore in the haven of your arms and be safe."

My, did Lorin like my confession of love! He tightened his hold and kissed me directly on my lips! As this was most unseemly behavior for us to be engaged in—I still in my bedclothes, unchaperoned, the rooster not yet crowed, and we not as yet married—I regretfully stepped away from him.

Lorin turned to go with his uniform in his arms.

I whispered, "Farewell, dearest. May God keep you safe."

"And you keep my gun in your pocket," he enjoined me.

Hundreds of bayonets caught the rays of the afternoon sun as it beat upon the assembled warriors outside the Mansion House that June afternoon. It was baking hot and the flies buzzed all about, but the soldiers stood at attention, riveted upon the words of their leader.

Across the road from the Mansion was an unfinished one-story frame house intended for Porter Rockwell, and upon its roof stood Uncle Joseph so that all could see and hear him. His voice rose in the sultry air. I dabbed my neck with my handkerchief and wished the soldiers could do the same.

"As soon as they have shed my blood they will thirst for the blood of every man in whose heart dwells a single spark of the spirit of the fullness of the gospel. The opposition of these men is moved by the spirit of the adversary of all righteousness." Despite the heat, a shiver ran across my flesh. I felt for the revolver tapping against my leg under my skirts. Brushing away the flies, I strained my ears to listen to his words.

"We are American citizens. We live upon a soil for the liberties of which our fathers imperiled their lives and spilt their blood upon the battlefield. Those rights, so dearly purchased, shall not be disgracefully trodden underfoot by lawless marauders without at least a noble effort on our part to sustain our liberties.

"Will you all stand by me to the death, and sustain at the peril of your lives, the laws of our country, and the liberties and privileges which our fathers have transmitted unto us, sealed with their sacred blood?"

Our thousands shouted, "Aye!" the female voices echoing from the army's edges. Every one of us stood a bit taller.

Uncle Joseph continued, "It is well. If you had not done it, I would have gone out there," and turning towards the river, he gestured towards the west, "and would have raised up a mightier people."

Then he drew his glistening sword towards the sun, and standing tall in majesty like a king, he declared, "I call God and angels to witness that I have unsheathed my sword with a firm and unalterable determination that this people shall have their legal rights, and be protected from mob violence, or my blood shall be spilt upon the ground like water and my body consigned to the silent tomb. While I live, I will never tamely submit to the dominion of cursed mobocracy. I would welcome death rather than submit to this oppression; and it would be sweet, oh, sweet, to rest in the grave rather than submit to this oppression, agitation, annoyance, confusion, and alarm upon alarm, any longer.

"God has tried you. You are a good people; therefore I love you with all my heart. Greater love hath no man than that he should lay down his life for his friends. You have stood by me in the hour of trouble, and I am willing to sacrifice my life for your preservation."

Sacrifice his life? Would it ever come to that? Would Uncle Joseph—and Father—be called upon to do that? Surely not! We could not do without them. Merciful God! Surely the Lord would not allow that to happen! That could never happen. They had always been watched over as with armies, yea legions of angels! No! Perish the thought! Never! No, never! That would be too cruel. I put the fearful notion firmly from my mind. Uncle Joseph was only teaching us a principle—that of sacrifice and devotion to country. He was only inspiring us with dedication. Was I prepared to fight for my constitutional rights as were my grandmothers? Could I hold a gun before me in defense of my liberties or for the safety of my loved ones? Could I? All my soul rose up and cried, "Yes! Yes! Yes!"

Chapter Twenty-seven

I went to work with a will. That afternoon Nauvoo was put under martial law. Whether due to exhaustion or peace of mind, we all slept much more soundly that night in our beds. Knowing the whole army paraded under my window, along the river, and upon each roadway leading to the city brought great comfort to me. No one was permitted into or out of the city without a pass. Guards stood upon every street and alley within the city. All the unclaimed arms within the city were put to use. I kept my gun in my pocket.

A few nights later, Father and Mother came home late from visiting the Mansion. Mother was suggesting, "Hyrum, perhaps we should take Joseph's advice and remove to Cincinnati."

Father sat down firmly in his chair. "Mary, I cannot leave my brother. I simply cannot do such a thing. What would my father say of me?"

"Not even when Joseph asks you to?" she asked gently as she lovingly hung up his hat. "For his sake?"

But Father shook his head. "No. I cannot do it. Do not ask it of me."

"Yes, Hyrum. I will support you." Mother turned to me and sighed. There was no moving Father when his mind was made up. He was even more obstinate than Mother. And she was the most determined woman I knew!

I had no desire at all to go away from Lorin, so I did not

attempt to persuade Father. Indeed, I asked instead if we might stay and move the wedding date forward.

"Fine!" said Father, putting his hands on the arms of his chair. "That's the soundest idea I've heard all night. You let me know when, and I'll perform the ceremony. That's all I ask. These fancy fripperies can be done without."

Mother protested, "Oh, Hyrum! It's our first wedding. Every girl needs a party!"

"Mother," I pleaded, "it's not as important to me anymore. Can we move the wedding forward?"

"All that work! And in a time of war? Do you know what you are asking?" said Mother.

I went to her and placed my hand on her arm. "Yes, I know. But I'm afraid. What if Lorin were killed?"

Mother placed her arms about me and rocked me back and forth like little Martha Ann. "Lovina, don't you know that God is watching over your soldier? Angels guard us all across the prairie. Nothing can happen to him."

"I suppose that's true," I sniffled. But those angels hadn't completely protected us from the mobs in the past. How we had suffered! Would it happen again? Would we all be killed?

The wedding plans were hastened. We made a shorter guest list and decided to dispense with half the cooking and leave off two rows of lace on my dress. I made my way to Brother Taylor's printing office the next day, determined to change the date of my wedding to the twenty-ninth of June, one week and one day away. It was the soonest Mother could prepare. I came upon several of the sisters in conversation. They hushed as I approached them.

"Is there any news?" I asked them uneasily.

They looked at one another, then one spoke. "If anyone ought to be worried, it should be you. It's rumored that Joseph Jackson is at Davidson Hibbard's and a posse has been sent to arrest him." The worst of all news! I had not heard more of him and thought him gone away for good. I felt fresh dismay rush through my being. "But would he dare to slip past the Legion guard?" I asked.

"That man would dare anything!" one sister responded.

"Why, I heard . . ."

Just then a soldier approached and stopped our talking. "Break it up, sisters! No gathering about in groups, no matter how juicy the gossip! Along with you."

An elderly sister chastised him. "Mind your manners! We were just giving Lovina Smith here fair warning of her peril. Joseph Jackson is loose in these parts. If you were doing your job properly, we would not need to warn her."

He bowed to us. "I beg your pardon, sister. We'd best offer her an escort as a precaution." And riding to the apothecary a few doors down, he yelled inside, "Brother Whitney! Walk along with this young lady and see that she arrives at her home safely!"

"Yes, sir!" Horace Whitney said with alacrity, emerging from the apothecary.

And indeed, I was eagerly and most gallantly escorted about on my errand by one of my former beaus. And under orders, too!

"Two men came from the governor this morning," Horace Whitney reported.

"You don't say!" I declared.

Horace helped me round a puddle and said, "His excellency is in Carthage."

"Maybe he will settle the mobs peacefully," I said as I lifted my skirts.

"Let us hope for that." Horace stopped. "Say, Lovina, look ahead. That isn't Jackson they have in custody, is it?"

"If it is, I hope they hold him fast!" I stopped walking too, afraid to go near him.

"Come on, girl, let's take a look!"

Horace grabbed my elbow and pulled me along the road until we had joined a whole group of spectators, orders to not gather about in crowds be hanged! Truly, it was our notorious Mr. Jackson under guard.

We met once again face to face. "Still about with the gentlemen, Lovina?" he sneered.

Crimson as a rose, I turned away from him. One of the soldiers stuck the butt of a gun against his back. "You'll not insult the ladies, Jackson."

Jackson stiffened.

"You deserve imprisonment and more, Mr. Jackson!" I retorted. "May God have mercy upon you, for truly I would not." My knees were knocking under my skirts as I said this to him.

"Come, Lovina," he said smoothly, "have a bit of pity on me. Cry friends for the sake of old times."

"Old times? Friends?" My voice rose to a nearly hysterical tone. "Have you no notion of friendship? You, who tore my reputation to tatters? You, who wish to murder my own father? You, who came to us as a spy sent by our greatest enemies? You know not the meaning of the word friendship!"

He turned to the gathered crowd and begged piteously, "I stand here a condemned man, all for unrequited love. You know not the fiery pangs of rejected passion. I stand before you as a forgotten suitor, cast out and degraded, bitter in my repudiation. Can you thus take pity upon this poor wretch that I am?" He held out his manacled arms before the crowd. Several, moved with pity at his impassioned speech, looked askance at me.

The devil! The liar! I knew not what to say. My jaw dropped but no words could come out, I was so shocked at his behavior. He knew the truth. I knew the truth. God knew the truth. But did the people of Nauvoo know the truth? Would they recall "Startling Disclosures?"

Horace spoke up for me. "No, Jackson. We cannot take pity on such as you. Take your lies to the devil with you."

"We know you for a liar," another yelled out in my support. How grateful I was for that!

So cunning was this rogue, ignoring my defense, that he reached into his pocket and pulled out his white silk kerchief and held it out to me. He pleaded, "Take it, Lovina. Take this pure white web as a token of my undying love for you."

Once again I was so stunned by his act, for an act it certainly was, that I could not answer him. I stepped back and felt for the gun in my pocket, trusting him nary a bit. He could grab me and hold me hostage. "You probably came here to kill me," I finally said in a choked voice.

"Your hard heart cuts me to the quick," he cried out and held the kerchief to his breast. He bowed his head as if in grief. Here, I confess I lost my good temper and did a most ungracious thing. When I told Mother later, she was horrified. I spat upon his boot. "Liar!" I yelled. "Never have you spoken or acted with love towards me. Do not attempt to do so now. You are only playing upon the sympathies of the crowd. This is not a melodrama!"

"Lovina!" he pleaded in apparent agony. My, he was desperate! He was a better tragedian than Thomas A. Lynde! We should have put him on the stage. Dropping the kerchief at my feet, he turned and was led away to his trial.

I was left to reassemble my feelings, his silk kerchief lying in the dust at my feet. The crowd stared at me.

"Take it, Lovina," said Horace Whitney. "Think what a good souvenir it will make for your grandchildren."

"How can you jest?" I asked Horace. Indeed, I could not imagine, for I was struck with nausea at Mr. Jackson's insinuations. "That man has accused me of loving him! And I did no such thing," I protested, in hopes that the crowd would understand.

"I remember a few times you preferred dancing with him to me," Horace laughed quietly.

With that reminder, my mortification quickly turned to anger. "How dare you remember that, Horace Whitney? Why, he tried to poison you!" And placing my shoe upon the kerchief, I ground it into the dust and stomped upon it. "That is what I think of yon Mr. Jackson!"

Horace attempted to lead me away before I made a further spectacle of myself. "Come on, Lovina, you're all het up and can't take a joke. Don't take that blackleg dandy so seriously. Nobody else does. He put on a good show, and we didn't even have to pay for it."

I could neither move nor take Horace's advice. I had become so angry and chagrined all at once, I was afraid I would faint.

"You look a bit peaked. Come on, I'll take you home now. I have to report back to duty." And Brother Whitney took me home.

Such a day I spent! Why, I could hardly do a lick of work for worry over the likes of Joseph Jackson. What would people say about me if he kept up his ridiculous stories? Would they hang him? Would they put him on trial before the circuit judge? What would be that verdict? How glad I was that at last he would come to justice and threaten the Smith family no longer!

At length, Father came home and made a report to us. "Ford is in Carthage and we sent him a packet of affidavits."

"What about Jackson?" I asked.

"He gave his testimony in lieu of a trial."

"In lieu of a trial?" I could not believe I had heard Father correctly.

"Yes, Lovina. After we produced affadavits against him, sworn and witnessed, he could do nothing else but give us the evidence we wanted." Father walked into his study and started to put away his papers.

I followed him, asking, "Didn't you jail him? Didn't you try him for murder?"

He turned back to me. "What for? We got our evidence."

I threw up my hands in dismay. "But he scared us! He's threatened our very lives!"

"What's in a threat?" Father turned away to his drawer.

"But . . ."

"The Savior said to love your enemies, bless them that curse you, do good to them that hate you, and pray for them who despitefully use you and persecute you."

I was silent as a tree. How could we do that? 'Twould be impossible for me to forgive that rascal all he had done.

Father looked up at me and added, "I'm sure that suffering the indignity of having to make a sworn confession of the truth to

Governor Ford and receiving kindness at the hands of his enemies was a much greater grievance to Mr. Jackson than putting a bullet through his head. Jackson is the proudest man I've ever met. He has a most peculiar temperament that seems incapable of forgiveness, but you can rest assured that justice was done and mercy applied. I have no feelings against him. 'Vengeance is mine, saith the Lord.'" He slapped his hand down upon his scriptures.

This was a hard doctrine.

Chapter Twenty-eight

At dark the next day—Saturday, the twenty-second of June—Father strode into the house with great purpose. "Pack me up, Mary; Joseph and I are going west. Do it quiet like, so as not to make it known generally."

I thought Mother would faint. "Hyrum!" she cried in shock.

"Whyever are you doing this?" asked Aunt Mercy, standing by Mother's side.

"Ford is under the influence of the mob and wants us in Carthage. As sure as we fall into their hands, we are dead men. We leave in an hour."

"Oh, Hyrum!"

"Don't fear, Mary; the Lord has opened the way. All they want is Joseph and me. They will come here and search, and not a hair on the heads of the Saints will be harmed. And Joseph and I will be safe. We'll go ahead to prepare a new gathering place in the Rocky Mountains."

"But, Hyrum—the west?" Mother said as she sat down in a chair. "Safe," she said to herself.

"Where's my brown shirt? And my old brown boots?" Father rushed to the bedroom to find them.

Then Mother got up and flew into action. Father would be safe. Aunt Mercy and Aunty Grinnels helped, running about for this and that. Mother plied Father with questions while we worked: How long would they be gone? What route would they take? Who would they stay with on the other side of the river? Could they cross in the dark? When would he write to assure her of his safety?

Aunty Grinnels packed Father some foodstuffs for the trip, and I sorted through his books. Father went through all his papers and sorted them into piles—one to burn, one to stay with us, and one to abandon. John was sent on errands back and forth to the Mansion House, and the younger children were told to stay in bed and out of the way. However, they could not sleep. So when all possible was prepared, we gathered in a family circle and offered up our prayers to that Father who made us. Only He could protect us now. Holding hands, we read the story of Lehi escaping from his enemies in Jerusalem from the Book of Mormon one last time together and then sang this hymn:

O God! our help in ages past, our hope for years to come,
Our shelter from the stormy blast, and our eternal home.
Under the shadow of thy throne; still may we dwell secure;
Sufficient is thine arm alone, and our defense is sure.

Then, one by one, Father left his blessing upon us.

At last it was my turn. When Father was done and I rose, I dared to ask, "Papa, what about my wedding?"

Father put his hands upon my shoulders and asked, "Can you forgive me for leaving?"

"We want you to go! But what should I do? I wanted you to marry us."

Turning away to gather just one more paper, he said, "Alas, there is no time tonight. We must go at once." He touched me on the head and enjoined me, "Lovina, you must be patient. Tomorrow I will write you a letter with my thoughts on the subject. If possible, perhaps I can slip back for your wedding, or you may come across. Or perhaps you will have to delay. I can make no plan tonight."

"That's all right. Your safety is far more important." "Lovina, this may be farewell for a long time hence." And with tears in his eyes he told me, "You've been a good daughter. Jerusha would have been proud of you. You've worked hard and served the younger ones, and you've been obedient. You're all I could have asked for. Tell Lorin to take good care of my daughter. Whether I meet him in this life or in the hereafter, I expect a good account from him." Taking me in his arms, he gave me a final squeeze. I nodded my head, for no words could leave me.

Uncle Joseph was waiting. "Sister Mary," he said, "don't feel bad. The Lord will take care of you, and he will deliver us, but I do not know how."

After Father said farewell once again, they walked to the river and disappeared into the clouds of darkness.

"Oh, keep him safe!" Mother pleaded with her Maker. Tears were on her cheeks. The little ones hung onto her skirt.

An hour later we received a message: "We are waiting for a boat. As soon as I am able, I will send for you and the children. Butler and Hodge are taking the *Maid of Iowa* to the North Landing for you and the children to board. You get on her and go to Ohio and wait there for word. Emma and the children are going, too."

I was at that moment placed in the most unpleasant circumstance of having to choose between two things dear to me. My home, father, mother, all my dreams, my past, my childhood— all gone away with those words, "We are going west!" Or I could choose the future I had planned with Lorin. Had things been normal, I would not have been under the necessity of making a choice. If we remained in Nauvoo, in leaving my family I would not have been separated from them. And what of my wedding, my party, my hopes and plans? Now none of my family would be there for my wedding! What would I do?

Mother protested, "How can we go to Cincinnati? It is but a moment's notice!"

"What about my wedding?"

That shocked Mother, because we would have to do without all her preparations. She concluded, "It will have to be delayed. There is not a moment to lose if we are to do as Hyrum says!"

"You mean that I ought to go with you?" Would that be my choice? Could I leave Lorin behind?

"What else can we do?" asked Aunt Mercy.

With resignation Mother stated, "We must do as your father says and leave, though I hate to be so far away from him."

Mother, Aunt Mercy, and Aunty Grinnels worked feverishly all that night. I sent word to Lorin that we were leaving and asked, "What should I do?"

He wrote back immediately, "Please don't leave! If you can bear to separate from your home and family, I'll find you a place to stay and we'll be married quickly. Forget the dress." The note was signed, "Dearest."

How I treasured his direction and worked all the harder for it! I kept my own things separate from the family's. Gone was my indecision. My future was with Lorin.

We were not finished packing, and come morning the city awoke to find that Uncle Joseph had fled. Upon almost every house came great consternation. In the streets the Saints and soldiers asked, "What of Brother Joseph's promise to stay and die for us?" They recalled his declaration: "You have stood by me in the hour of trouble, and I am willing to sacrifice my life for your preservation!"

"In our hour of trouble, has he left us to the wolves?" they wondered. Every man's faith was shaken right to its foundations. People milled about in groups as was forbidden, talking, crying, exclaiming, wondering what was to become of them. Others hastened to run away too. Was Brother Joseph deserting the faith? Would he leave his flock to perish? Was he a true shepherd?

But Mother and Aunt Mercy continued to work, telling all who called what the Lord had whispered to Uncle Joseph. When we were almost done, John came back from an errand to the Mansion and said that they hadn't packed at all. That sent Mother across the way posthaste.

"That Emma!" she said when she returned. "She says she's not going. She's promised to stay here and fight the mobs. Well, Mercy, what do we do now?"

Our dilemma was solved by the appearance of Porter Rockwell with a note from Father that read, "I said I'd write any change of plans immediately. I believe that it would be feasible for you to travel west with Joseph and me. What do you say, Mary? Will you come west?

"We spent a long night in a leaky skiff, but by the grace of God we made it safely across to Iowa. I'm afraid some of my things became quite wet. I miss you with all my bleeding heart. Come west. Love to the children. Hyrum."

"Now what shall we do?" asked Mother.

Aunt Mercy suggested, "Let's go talk to Sister Emma. She's probably received the same request."

When they returned Mother was saying, "Poor Emma, not feeling well, can't be expected to go west. I think she should be put to bed. She looks about to collapse. All those men are badgering her as if she were the head of the Church, saying they want Joseph back before the Saints lose faith in him!"

Aunt Mercy agreed. "Joseph and Hyrum run away! They went because the spirit prompted them to. I'll tell them a thing or two!"

Mother wrote a note to Father telling him that they would join him.

John called from the yard, "Mother! Mother, there's a posse coming!"

Reaching out to draw him to her, Mother said, "Come inside. They might hunt for your father. I want us together."

Our packing was temporarily forgotten. As sure as the sun would rise, they came knocking on our door and asked for Father. "He's gone away," said Mother boldly, allowing them in. She wouldn't have done that had Father been home. My, we were glad he had escaped!

"We'll search the premises," said their leader. They showed us the order from Governor Ford, pushed past us, and proceeded to do so. "He's nowhere here, Major," a soldier said. I remembered other times when men had come to search our house for Father. My knees had shaken, my mouth had grown dry, and my heart had beaten violently. Remembering this, I held the young children tightly to me so they would feel secure. I was glad of Lorin's revolver and excessively comforted to know that Father was safe across the waters. It was worth giving up my wedding for that comfort.

The men went out and began to search the town. When they couldn't find them and were sure the people were telling the truth when they said Brother Joseph and Brother Hyrum were gone, they began to curse and swear and make themselves unpleasant. "If you — — Mormons don't give them two up, the governor will bring down the state troops and invade Nauvoo! We'll guard this city three years if necessary!"

They left behind a Mr. Yates to keep a lookout and returned to give the governor the news. Yates rode up and down the streets of Nauvoo, his gun waving in the air, yelling, "You — — Mormons had better give them leaders of yours up! If you don't, not a brick will be left standing in Nauvoo! Governor Ford will bring in the whole state militia to do the job." All the people were in a frenzy of fear, and the sisters rushed into their houses to pack up a few belongings for a quick escape.

"Occupation! Invasion! Even the Nauvoo Legion cannot combat the armies of the whole state of Illinois! How could Brother Joseph desert us at such a time? How could he?" people said. At this turn of events, several delegations of men took skiffs and secretly rowed across the river to persuade the two leaders to return. Aunt Emma sent a letter asking him to return. Knowing the terror of the people, she promised that she would not leave, but would stay and fight or die. She and several of the brethren became quite zealous in their feelings.

"Humbug!" said Mother and Aunt Mercy. "Joseph wouldn't leave if it weren't for a good reason."

"Wouldn't the Lord protect them if they returned?" I asked

timidly.

"I don't know. I don't know," said Mother. She sounded as if her faith was sorely tried. With all her heart she longed for Father's escape. But she was also dog tired, and she knew the faith of the Saints hung in the balance. She sat down to think.

Then she got up and went back to packing. If Father said so, she was going west. Though it was the Sabbath, we all had pressing work to do. Mother reorganized things into new piles. When she was halfway done, word came across the river that Father was returning to submit to law. All work stopped. We knew what that meant. We looked at one another, afraid to voice the word—jail. Would the Lord protect Father if he did not flee west?

The change in plans necessitated our washing his white shirts and brushing his good suit so he would look impressive before the judge. If that would help, we were willing to make his shirts whiter than white. We gave up on the packing and left the piles about, wondering what lay in store for us.

While I was outdoors hanging Father's laundry on the line, I saw the skiff coming, travelling slowly along the fiery path of the setting sun. It dipped beneath the horizon as Father and Uncle Joseph docked. But Uncle Joseph just sat there with his head bowed. I'd never seen him so stooped, not even when little Don Carlos died. He could not seem to get out of the boat and sat there like he was glued to the river. Father came up to me and asked when I planned to be married.

"It depends on the circumstances. Lorin's willing."

Placing his pack by the doorstep, Father said wearily, "If you want me to marry you, it will have to be tonight."

"Tonight! Oh, Papa!"

"I'll tell your mother to be ready," he said as he turned to go indoors to find her. He waved at Uncle Joseph to join him.

"Oh, thank you, Papa! Tell Mother not to fuss," I called. Then I threw off my apron and ran to find my dearest.

Chapter Twenty-nine

"You have taken one another by the right hand in token of the covenants you will now enter into in the presence of God and these witnesses," said Father as we stood before him amongst our piles of packing in the family kitchen. Lorin wore his Legion uniform, now dusty and soiled, and I wore my Christmas dress once again. Mother had cleaned away as much as was possible, and Father had shaved and done his business and put his suit on. The children were scrubbed and brushed and allowed to stay up for the family party, excited to have Father home and the family gathered. Uncle Joseph, Aunt Emma, and Grandmother had come over, and Lucy Walker stood by my side. Lorin's brother William had gone on the steamer to Burlington to bring a witness to Carthage for the coming trial, so he couldn't be there. The remainder of our intended guests were absent.

"Lorin Walker, do you take Lovina Smith as your lawfully-wedded wife, and do you of your own free will and choice covenant as her companion and lawfully-wedded husband that you will cleave unto her; that you will observe all the laws, covenants, and obligations pertaining to the holy state of matrimony; and that you will love, honor, and cherish her as long as you both shall live?"

Lorin squeezed my right hand tightly in his right hand as he looked at my father and promised, "Yes."

Father smiled, satisfied.

When he had spoken the same words to me, I answered, "I do." My voice trembled as I contemplated the enormity of the covenant I was making before God.

Father went on, "By virtue of the legal authority vested in me as an elder of the Church of Jesus Christ of Latter-day Saints, I pronounce you, Lorin Walker and Lovina Smith, husband and wife, legally and lawfully wedded for the period of your mortal lives. May God bless your union with joy in your posterity and a long life of happiness together, and may he enable you to keep sacred the covenants you have made. These blessings I invoke upon you in the name of the Lord Jesus Christ. Amen."

Tears came to my eyes. I turned to look at my dearest.

"You may kiss each other as husband and wife."

Oh! I had forgotten that! Blushing furiously, I closed my eyes and turned up my head. When nothing happened, I opened them. Lorin was as embarrassed as I with all the family looking on.

"Go on, kiss her!" hissed my brother.

So Lorin did.

Then the family surrounded us and added to my kiss several others. Mother brought out a cake she had procured from some mysterious source. After tendering my farewells to Grandmother and Uncle Joseph and Aunt Emma, who with the press of affairs could not remain, Lucy led me off to change into the lacy fripperies that I had been preparing just for this occasion. No one would see them now but Lorin and the family! Father, John, and old George made up Lorin's wedding party. We could hear them talking in the next room, and then there was silence.

Mother and Aunt Mercy came into the room to admire me and to show me to bed. "I'd like a private word with my daughter first," said Mother. "Do you mind?" The others left us alone.

"Lovina, I intended to have this talk with you before your wedding, but with things as they are . . ."

"Yes, Mother?"

"There are woman things you should know. Lovina, you've

been to the farm and . . ."

"Yes, Mother?" What was it she wanted to say? I'd never known her to be shy before—gracious, but never reticent.

"Lovina, I want you to have joy and rejoicing in your posterity."

Was that all? I reassured her, "Oh, Lorin and I intend to have many children!"

"I'm sure you'll find a way. That's all I have to say." Mother stood up and, greatly agitated, added, "Remember the farm and remember to have joy. That's all." And she left the room.

Lucy joined me and we opened the door to the bedroom. Lorin was already in the bed—asleep! So much for my party!

I crawled under my side of the mosquito netting and gestured for Lucy to be quiet. "Bring me some cake and then go rest. I'll not waken him," I whispered.

"Oh, Lovina—your party," bemoaned Lucy. "My brother!"

"Poor Lorin has hardly slept for a week. We'll have our own party later. Let him rest," I whispered.

Indeed, my Lorin looked like a log half submerged in the river. I closed his mouth and smoothed back his hair from his brow. Most all of it had grown back, and the part that hadn't served to remind me of the prayer I had offered four months earlier, kneeling in that very room, asking the Lord to bless me to have Lorin for my own. Then I had been chilled, and I had tucked a quilt about me as I watched the river unfreeze. Now my heart felt not cold, but warm with the fulfillment of the Lord's promise. Lorin was mine.

Chapter Thirty

The family allowed us to sleep late, but there was so much noise and sunshine about that we could not help but awaken. Lorin shook my shoulder. "Lovina!"

I opened a sleepy eye at him.

"Are you angry with me, dearest?"

I rolled over. "Angry? Because you were asleep?"

"Yes. Whoever heard of a bridegroom missing his wedding night?"

"We are at war. That qualifies as an unusual circumstance."

"I love you," he whispered. "Come here." I went into his arms and felt heaven. Truly the sunshine streaming through my window portended a wonderful new day.

"Vina, Papa's leaving!" my sister called. Throwing on a robe over my fancy bedclothes, I dashed down the stairs.

An indescribable sadness shadowed each countenance, and I had never seen Father so despondent. How could there be so much joy in this world and yet so much sorrow, all at once? Why did they have to take my father away? He had done nothing wrong.

Father solemnly climbed upon his white horse, Sam. Other men were waiting for him upon their horses. I could see down Main Street that people were lined up along the road to watch them ride away, early as it was. Many were in tears, as was Father. I'd never seen him so sorrowful to leave us—not when he rode to

Carthage the month before, and not even when they jailed him in Missouri.

When they had gone, Mother went to bed with her sorrow. Sending Father to trial for destroying the press was much harder than sending him with his brother the month before. This time he too was on trial. The question hung in the air: Would they return? I cooked Lorin some corn mush and fed some to the children, then sent him off to work. I found much consolation in my new wifely duties. I was truly a wife now! I moved my trunk and wardrobe into a room in the Mansion and made a bit of a home for Lorin and me. How proud I was of my new quilts and sheets! And Mother gave me a small watercolor she had brought from England to hang on my wall. I moved Lorin's few things into the room and mended and straightened out his clothes tenderly. I held my half-finished wedding dress in my arms, and then hung it away for better days.

"Some soldiers is come to take our arms!" Jane Manning cried out in the hallway.

I rushed from my new room. Surely this was not true! How would we defend ourselves from the mob? "Remember Far West!" hung upon my heart. What more could they do to us? We had been slandered and bullied and degraded. Would they also leave us defenseless?

I saw Lorin drive a wagon out to help collect guns and powder from the troops scattered about. It was only the state arms that they could lay claim to. I breathed a sigh of relief. Only God knew how grateful we were that we owned plenty of other ammunition.

Father and Uncle Joseph returned to Nauvoo shortly after the arrival of the division of state troops. Father seemed in much brighter spirits. The state troops under Captain Dunn were orderly and respectful and earned a degree of our trust. When the weapons were collected and locked into the basement of the Masonic Hall, Lorin came back briefly to confer with Uncle Joseph about what to do to cover the loss of the state-owned munitions. We were now short over two hundred weapons. Turning to me, Uncle Joseph took my hand and asked me a question. "When I heard you covenant to cleave unto your husband, did you mean it with all your heart?"

"Yes," I said in considerable surprise.

"Come what may?"

I looked into those prophetic eyes that knew me so well and could see right through my very soul. "You know that for the truth," I replied. I could not imagine not keeping that covenant. He squeezed my fingers. "I am going to ask Lorin to do one last thing for me. It will prove difficult. Will he have your unqualified support?"

Uncle Joseph looked terribly solemn and serious. I swallowed and agreed. What was he asking?

He turned away, satisfied. "That is good. Emma, come here." Then Uncle Joseph took one of Aunt Emma's hands and one of Lorin's hands and said to Aunt Emma, "Woman, behold thy son." And turning to Lorin, he said, "Behold thy mother." He placed Aunt Emma's hand in Lorin's. His words mirrored those spoken by Jesus on the cross, recorded in the New Testament book of John. What did Uncle Joseph mean? Were we to be as his children? What was so hard about that?

Tears were in Lorin's eyes as we climbed to our room together. I was anxious to see how he would like our new home, but he scarcely saw it. Lorin sat upon the bed and cried with wracking sobs like grown men do when they cry. Not even my caresses brought him comfort. "He's going to die, Lovina. Your father and Brother Joseph are going to their deaths. That's the last time I'll see Brother Joseph alive. He knows," Lorin sobbed.

"No, no, no! He'll come back, dearest. Father was more hopeful this time. The troops were quite friendly. Try to have hope. The Lord will watch over them both. Last time they were fine. Aunt Emma assured us they will be fine."

He would not be comforted. "You heard Brother Joseph. He gave Sister Emma into our keeping. It was final."

What Lorin said struck me oddly, and I dared not reply for

fear of giggling in the face of his sorrow.

Lorin looked up at me. "Lovina! How can you be so unfeeling as to laugh at your own father's death? Don't you understand?"

I could not help it and lay back on the bed. "I'm not laughing at that. 'Tis the idea of Aunt Emma being in anyone's keeping but Uncle Joseph's. She is the most strong-headed woman I know, next to Mother. Can you imagine her listening to *us*?"

"No. I cannot." Lorin stood up and began to plead with me, saying, "Lovina, you've got to face what will come . . ."

But I replied, "Come, Lorin, smile. Let's say our very first prayer in our new home and fill it with some measure of joy. Father would have it that way. We'll pray for them."

That met both of our needs. We knelt, and Lorin offered our first prayer in our new home.

During the next few days we all prayed anxiously for the brethren's safety. As Lorin was one of those to redistribute the weapons, I did not see him often. But the Mansion was a hive of activity which kept us girls so busy that I barely noticed he was gone. Messengers and messages flew back and forth between Carthage and Nauvoo. Every hour brought fresh news of the progress of the trial. People reported that Joseph Jackson was still in Carthage and in league with Levi Williams, that notorious Mormon-hater. Jackson boasted that he himself was a "true prophet," and claimed that within days the blood of "Holy Joe" and Hyrum would be spilt. When I heard that story, I thought him the most ungrateful being on this earth. Had we not held him in the palms of our hands and given him his freedom? Had we not done him good in return for his evil?

Others said the Carthage Grays had behaved with the most unmilitary discipline imaginable—so much so that their behavior was not repeated to the ladies. All of the apostates were gathered in the mob and were also insolent and spoke freely before others about spilling blood. However, the governor pledged his protection with his faith.

On Tuesday the twenty-fifth, Aunt Emma received a message

from Uncle Joseph that read:

"Dear Emma. — I have had an interview with Governor Ford, and he treats us honorably. Myself and Hyrum have been again arrested for treason because we called out the Nauvoo Legion; but when the truth comes out we have nothing to fear. We all feel calm and composed.

"This morning Governor Ford introduced myself and Hyrum to the militia in a very appropriate manner, as General Joseph Smith and General Hyrum Smith. There was a little mutiny among the Carthage Greys, but I think the Governor has and will succeed in enforcing the laws. I do hope the people of Nauvoo will continue pacific and prayerful.

"Governor Ford has just concluded to send some of his militia to Nauvoo to protect the citizens, and I wish that they may be kindly treated. They will co-operate with the police to keep the peace. The Governor's orders will be read in the hearing of the police and officers of the Legion, as I suppose.

"3 o'clock. — The Governor has just agreed to march his army to Nauvoo, and I shall come along with him. The prisoners, all that can, will be admitted to bail. I am as ever, Joseph Smith."

I took the letter over to Mother, who was indignant that Hyrum was arrested for treason, though the tone of the message calmed her fears a bit. It was outrageous! What kind of a governor was Ford? He knew why the Nauvoo Legion had been called out. Treason was a more serious charge for which they could not be released on bail.

When the brethren had come up for trial for the *Expositor* incident, bail was put high so as to keep the prisoners there, and the officials necessary to the defense were ofttimes inaccessible. But the brethren raised the bail by dint of great sacrifice. So they rearrested Uncle Joseph and Father for treason. It was clearly a trap. The mobs were determined to keep them in Carthage. They moved Father and Uncle Joseph to the jail and locked them in. Several brethren stayed with Uncle Joseph and Father in jail; others returned to Nauvoo, reporting that Uncle Joseph had told a few of the officers of the mob armies that they thirsted for his blood. He made a prophecy that they would see enough blood to fully satisfy them if they killed him. What did this mean? Would all of our blood be spilt on the ground? Or was this an event that would occur at some later date? I hid from the thought of some blackened-faced ruffian, thirsting for my blood. I feared that if I thought too much on it, I would never again sleep nights.

Another report came in that the "anties" had confided that they had no evidence against the church leaders and the law couldn't hurt them, but powder and ball could. What were we to think? Could Governor Ford control them? Could he be trusted? What would we do if he turned against us with the state troops? Fight? Flee across the river?

Others heard that Joseph Jackson said if they didn't retain "Old Joe" on that charge, he had eighteen others against him. Jackson said, "They won't get out alive!" Pointing to his pistols, he said, "The balls are in here that will decide his case."

I felt that dreadfully when I heard it. That same sick feeling I had when Jackson was arrested came over me. How could a man be so wicked? Was he demented in his brain? Truly he was the wickedest man in the world, as he had claimed.

Chapter Thirty-one

After those disclosures made by the returning brethren, we placed little faith in the promises of Governor Ford. He had proved himself to be a man without principle or charity for the helpless, and no true friend to the Mormons.

Every man held onto his arms and said his prayers. I kept my gun close to my side.

Word next came that Uncle Joseph had been granted a lengthy interview with Governor Ford, who had again assured their safety. But the hundreds of soldiers about Carthage were determined to see blood. Several of the brethren heard boasts to that effect while in Carthage. The governor turned a deaf ear when they apprised him of the boasts.

The next day, Thursday the twenty-seventh of June, Aunt Emma received two letters express from Uncle Joseph. Every time a letter arrived for her, people came to read it. They were not able to be very personal on that account, but that was not his intent. One, received about noon on that day, contained direction to Brother Dunham, who had charge of the Legion, and instructions for our behavior in the event that the governor did visit. While assuring us that there would be no extermination order and that a part of the troops under the governor would not mutiny, he added:

"There is one principle which is eternal; it is the duty of all men to protect their lives and the lives of the household, whenever necessity requires, and no power has a right to forbid it, should the last extreme arrive, but I anticipate no such extreme, but caution is the parent of safety. - Joseph Smith

"P.S. — Dear Emma, I am very much resigned to my lot, knowing I am justified, and have done the best that could be done. Give my love to the children and all my friends, and all who inquire after me; and as for treason, I know that I have not committed any. May God bless you all. Amen."

This letter was not so positive as the other. It gave additional credence to the stories the brethren told of the threats of the mobs. We all felt like tightened violin bows. I wondered how Aunt Emma could bear all the suspense, loving Uncle Joseph as she did. She must have felt it more deeply than I. Often I wondered if I were in her position, and Lorin jailed, could I behave with as much command and fortitude as my Aunt Emma? She was a wall of strength in this time of crisis. Though in a sick condition herself, she gave and gave, offering her home and her solace to others, and practically running the whole city. I persuaded her to rest, yet she would not whilst there was anything she could do in behalf of Uncle Joseph. She could not be at ease in the crisis.

A few hours later, Aunt Emma received the following postscript from Uncle Joseph: "I just learned that the Governor is about to disband his troops, all but a guard to protect us and the peace, and come himself to Nauvoo and deliver a speech to the people. This is right I suppose."

Most all of the brethren came home shortly after that. Brother Wheelock came right to Aunt Emma with memorized messages for her to hear, and they were delivered to her privately. We wondered what they were, if they were very different from his public messages, but Aunt Emma kept them to herself.

Then Brother Wheelock took others of the family and even Lucy Walker into the room and gave them messages. None were for me; I had had my counsel. I went home to see if Mother had any messages.

I found Mother with a full heart brimming over with tears.

Father had sent word to her that she was the finest woman on the earth and that it was a humble privilege to have had the care of her. He wished her to stay close to Heavenly Father always and to follow the twelve apostles, those who had the keys of the kingdom. Father gave his love to all his children and enjoined them to do good for evil always. That sounded like Father.

I stayed a while to talk of the news. It felt so good to be in my own home once again! I had missed both Father and Mother. Though I had worked hard on my new little room, Lorin had been with me so seldom that I could not feel it to be a real home as yet.

My brothers called from the yard, "They're coming, the troops are coming! We're being invaded!"

At once we put down our work and rushed outdoors. Down the hill came bouncing lights—the lights of sword tips glinting in the broiling sun—many of them, coming this way! I clutched my apron tightly in my hands and wrung it. Would that the Lord would have mercy on us! Governor Ford was here at last.

Our soldiers galloped about the streets crying, "Keep the peace. Go about your business. Do not gather in groups."

Immediately we went indoors. I felt for my revolver and stayed by my family, ready to defend them if necessary. Governor Ford and his officers went right to the Mansion House and went inside. I thought of Lorin's promise to Uncle Joseph to be a son to Aunt Emma, and my promise to support him. I had promised. Was this what was meant? Was I to go to her, I asked myself? Was that now my place, not with my own family? I thought of how Aunt Emma had borne up under pressure despite her sickness. She had been like a fortress in the midst of the battle, like a tower of strength upon the fortress. Could she bear up now?

I crossed the road.

There were state troops at ease outside the yard of the Mansion. As I passed them by there were a few whispered comments upon my person, but I paid them no attention. Governor Ford was upstairs in the front room with his party of men. I stopped Jane Manning and inquired of her what had happened during my absence.

"Those men is up in the front room, practicin' fancy speeches. Sent Porter Rockwell up to fetch his hat, and they done shut up like secrets. I don't like them men. They up to no good."

I found Aunt Emma following the governor's orders, as directed by Uncle Joseph, to assemble the people in front of the Mansion. Major-General Dunham of the Legion was with her in consultation.

Hundreds of Saints gathered in the road, and the governor and his party came out. State troops surrounded them like wolves around a fire. I slipped out the back way and crossed the road to the stable, went behind it and came out by the landing. If the troops caused trouble, I did not wish to be in the center of the crowd.

The governor began his speech. "A great crime has been done by destroying the Expositor press and placing the city under martial law, and a severe atonement must be made, so prepare your minds for the emergency."

I thought, along with all the other women who heard the speech, that surely the people of this state must be without conscience if they could elect a man so deaf to the rights of virtuous women as to condemn the destruction of a piece of work such as the *Expositor*! However, we kept the peace as Brother Joseph wished.

Ford went on to say, "Depend on it, a little more misbehavior from the citizens, and the torch, which is already lighted, will be applied, and the city may be reduced to ashes, and extermination would inevitably follow; and it gives me great pain to think that there is danger of so many innocent women and children being exterminated. If anything of a serious character should befall the lives or property of the persons who are prosecuting your leaders, you will be held responsible."

We were stunned at this unfair speech! That the governor of a state in a land that boasted of liberty for all would make such a speech! We who had behaved with so much forbearance in the face of every possible provocation? No other people on the face of the earth would have done so! And to be so boldly accused of misbehavior? Unfair!

It was a testimony of our desire for law and order that we did not at that time rise up and overthrow such a man, but bore his insults with meekness and silently returned to our homes. We could have done otherwise.

I slipped behind the stable once again. All was silent behind its wall. Were the horses within suddenly gone? I turned to look at the river and saw no birds. The water was still as glass, as if the river had stopped in its course. The branches on the trees were drooping and the plants in the garden went limp. The grass itself lay flat as if in sorrow. Even the flies were absent. Why? Why was nature so still and solemn?

A great fear took hold of me as I crossed to the Mansion. I found Lorin there, searching for me in our room, and I ran into his arms. "Oh, Lorin! All nature is in mourning!"

"Lovina, what are you saying?"

"The earth is silent. Did you not witness it?"

"It's Brother Joseph. It's happened." Lorin sat down as if crushed by a heavy weight.

I sought to reassure him, saying, "Nothing can happen to him, Lorin. He's a prophet of God. Aunt Emma said he'll come back. She must know."

At length he answered, "It's because he is a prophet that nature mourns at his pain. One can only pray that you are right and he is not taken from us. I don't know how we could get on without him."

Lorin got up and went outside to witness the passing of the state troops out of Nauvoo. They performed dazzling exercises—passes and guards, cuts and thrusts, as if marching in a Fourth of July parade. There were no crowds lining the streets for this parade, for a deep and ponderous sadness moved over the city like a fog off the river.

Later it was found that the troops stopped at the temple and desecrated the baptismal font, breaking off the ears of the oxen. But we were relieved once again to have our city to ourselves under the protection of troops respectful of virtue, womanhood, and truth.

As the sun passed behind the edge of the world, a darkness that seemed thicker than night settled upon the land. It was a darkness felt as well as perceived, not unlike the days after Christ the Lord died upon the cross. Occasionally the whole world would light up with great flashes of lightning from the eternal realms. Who and what were those bolts striking? I thought of Lorin out there on the plains in nothing but a rough tent, exposed to the night. Would the lightning strike the upright of heart, or those of evil intent?

What before had been silence, now became bedlam. The wind whistled through the alleyways and open windows. The dogs howled to the lost moon and stars. The cattle bellowed in their barns and the cats prowled. The birds flew about and made noise. Even the chickens would not settle, but crowed and cackled like a fox was upon them. On such a night, who could find rest?

A knock came upon my bedroom door. It was Lucy Walker, now my sister-in-law. "I cannot sleep. Where is Lorin?"

"He's on patrol again. The mob may come upon us at any moment." I rose to take her hand.

"I fear that. Perhaps that is why I cannot rest."

I did not tell her Lorin's fears that Uncle Joseph was dead. We knelt in prayer together, but found that we had no utterance. No words could leave our heavy hearts. Truly the forces of darkness reigned that night! What had happened?

"Stay with me, Lucy. Don't leave me," I begged my friend. We waited quietly together, huddled on my bed through the hours of that night. Neither of us wished to be alone.

Suddenly the hot night air was rent with a cry of heartbreak. Lucy and I clutched one another in the darkness. What could it be? Had something happened? Had Ford returned to exterminate us? Was someone murdered? It sounded frightful!

Together we tiptoed to the door of my little room and peered out. "What is it?" we cried. "What is it?" we cried again fearfully. We had no answer. Step by step, we went down the stairs to the front hall. Several of the brethren were there. We stopped, unable to go any further for fear of what we would learn.

"He's dead," they whispered. And then I knew that Lorin had known the truth when he said that Brother Joseph would die.

One of the men looked upon me with great pity. "Hyrum, too."

I felt an absolute darkness engulf me and mercifully knew no more. Lucy and I both fainted with the shock.

Chapter Thirty-two

I was carried to my bed and lay there in a state of insensibility until Lorin returned and found me. The whole household was paralyzed; not a stitch of work was done nor a sound was heard save that of weeping. The hens' eggs lay on the ground ungathered, and in the kitchen the milk curdled in its pail. All were stricken with the agony of overwhelming and debilitating grief. The thought crossed my mind to go to my family for comfort, yet I could not sufficiently rouse myself to do so. I lay numbly upon my bed.

Lorin bathed my face and brushed back my hair, all the while talking to me gently. "Brother Richards and Hamilton from Carthage have brought home the bodies. We went out to meet them. Hamilton was kind enough to wash them and build boxes. It's so hot today that they had to cover them over with branches. Brother Huntington is downstairs preparing them for burial."

My heart was touched as Lorin served me, and my tears began to flow. He continued to wipe my face with a cool, wet rag.

"Lucy has gone to William and Olive. Brother Richards talked to the people. Almost the whole city came out to hear him."

"How did it happen?"

"'Twas over quickly and they did not suffer. A mob stormed the jail, which was inadequately protected. Ford left them in the charge of the Carthage Grays, of all troops! Like Pilate, Ford's infamy will stink through the centuries for that deed. The mob was painted black. They attacked from both the stairs and the window of the jail." And here Lorin took my hand for comfort. "Your father died first from a shot through the door. He said, 'I am a dead man.' To save the lives of the others, Brother Joseph jumped through the window and was killed. It was over quickly, and the mob ran away. Brother Richards escaped the bullets unharmed."

I roused myself to ask, "Was anyone else killed?" Oh, that this calamity might not come upon any other household, that none other be left orphaned as I.

"Brother Taylor was wounded. All the other brethren had been chased away." Lorin leaned down and kissed me. "Lovina, you still have me. We have each other."

"Oh, Lorin, how is it that you can comfort me when you must feel the pain too?"

"I do feel it, like a great empty rock in my soul's center that I must drag about with me. But I was prepared for it. You were not. I have shed my tears."

I remembered.

"Can you bear it if I do Brother Joseph a service and leave you?"

"Aunt Emma?"

"Yes."

"How does she bear it?" I asked. Aunt Emma had been a bastion of strength in every trial. Could she bear this one, this last, final test? I began to weep for her.

"Do you remember the day the wall of the Seventies Hall blew down? It was strong and straight and tall. One thought it impregnable. And then the winds came and blew it down. The wind has come to Sister Emma. She has collapsed like the bricks and mortar. It will be our job to rebuild that wall and care for it. That is the charge Brother Joseph gave to us."

I rose from my bed. There were worse things than my own heartache. I was needed. "Go to her, Lorin. I'm going to Mother. She too may need me, and I know I need her!"

My own mama was gone home years ago, but Mother had found her own place in my heart. I belonged by her side in this hour.

My little sisters could not understand. "Where's Papa?" they asked me. What could I say? I gathered them in my arms and wept for them. How I knew their pain! I was but ten years old when Mama died, and how I missed her! And now these poor mites would grow up without their papa. He was torn from their sides by hatred. It was not fair!

Perhaps the greatest service I could render in this hour was to teach my sisters and brothers the meaning of death, to save Mother the task of preparing them for the scene that lay ahead. "Papa's gone home to heaven and the angels," I explained. "He's with our mama."

"But they brought him on the wagon. We saw it."

How could I tell them? Then I said, "That is his body. His spirit is with God. Remember when the kitten died? It didn't move or breathe. We put it in the box and buried it under the tree."

"Won't Papa breathe?"

"Not until the day of resurrection. His body will be waiting until then."

"Won't he come back?"

I wept. "No, he won't come back." Oh, how could we bear it?

They came and told us that we could view our loved ones with the family and a few friends. The crowds were expected the next day. Holding tightly to the children, I crossed the road once again, determined to be stalwart for their sakes. Lorin and some of the brethren held Aunt Emma. She could not bear to enter the room. I marveled at her incapacity. Where was her tower of strength? I went in with the children. The bodies lay side by side, those two giants of men who were my father and uncle. So close had they been in life, and now close in death. I hesitated to go near, but little Sarah dragged me forward.

"He's cold, Lovina! He's cold like the kitten. Papa! Papa! Papa!"

I could no longer hold out when I witnessed their distress, but fell upon my papa and wept with the sorrow of the ages.

Alas, his life was truly gone. His corpse lay disfigured by the hand of darkness. How could they? How could they do this to my papa? I could see the wound beside his nose—he did not look natural. I looked at Uncle Joseph's remains. His shoulder was stained with blood from his wounds. Oh, Lord God! How could we bear this calamity? How could God let this happen?

Grandmother Smith came in and when she saw her sons, sank back, saying, "My God, my God, why hast thou forsaken this family?"

Indeed, we felt forsaken. Aunt Emma was carried out insensible. She had endured too much.

"Why does Papa have a hole in his face, Lovina?" asked my sisters.

"Because bad men shot him when he testified of the truth. Remember that, Sarah and Jerusha and Martha. Father died for the truth."

Lorin took the girls to look at Uncle Joseph, who looked less unnatural. "Lovina's right. Look upon your uncle's face. Does he look sad? Or lonely?"

"He looks happy," they agreed.

"He and your father have gone somewhere where they are happy. They can see you and want you to be good and come to them when you die."

Uncle Joseph's countenance was serene and at rest. I felt a quiet peace at last steal over me as I gazed at him. Perhaps they were there with us in our hour of need, to comfort the Saints and continue their work for us. Perhaps they were with Grandfather Smith, Uncle Don Carlos, Uncle Alvin, and the children of the family who had died. Uncle Joseph often preached and taught that we would be surrounded by friends and loved ones when we died. Were they all, too, here in this family gathering?

Uncle Samuel took sick right after the viewing, and Uncle William was far away in Philadelphia. Grandma went to work nursing Uncle Samuel.

Throughout the next day, thousands walked past the two bodies. Up and down the river, steamboats brought people anxious to see the dead prophet and his brother. Children were kept indoors because of the crowds. We remained upstairs, witnesses to the sounds of their distress. They were but echoes of our own.

We followed the procession to the cemetery and stopped to hear the words of comfort given by Brother Phelps. Usually words were offered to a grieving family and a few friends; but these words were administered under the inspiration of the almighty to a whole people grieving. Oh, how many people loved the prophet and his brother! Both friends and strangers stood within the shadow of the temple.

Feelings ran high. The people had witnessed for themselves the destruction done by the mob. They had been betrayed by those officials of the state upon whom they had relied for protection. Some wanted vengeance. Others, like myself, were beyond that emotion and sought only solace.

In lively words, Brother Phelps taught us that vengeance would be the Lord's, and that we were to stand and watch him avenge us of our enemies. Wars, calamities, and strife would vex our nation for their rejection of Joseph Smith the Prophet.

He told of the greatness of Uncle Joseph, who had said, "You never knew me."

Then Brother Phelps said, "I will say that he has done more in fifteen years to make the truth plain, open the way of life, and carry glad tidings to the meek than all Christendom had done in fifteen hundred years." He told of how Uncle Joseph "came to bring the Book of Mormon to light from its angel-guarded home in the hill Cumorah. He came to establish our church upon earth, upon the pure and eternal principles of revelation. He came to punish vice, and praise virtue; he came to darken the dungeons of lust, and light up the mansions of love; he came to expel the errors of the ages and teach men to walk in the light of the Lord.

"He is dead, but he lives; he is absent from us, but at home in heaven. Tell the world, and let eternity bear record, that the great name of Joseph Smith will go down to unborn worlds and up to sanctified heavens, and gods, with all his shining honors and endless fame as stars in his crown, while the infamy of his persecutors can only be written in their ashes."

As our wagon slowly passed by the multitude of mourners, I thought of the men who had done the deed—those who once had worshipped with us, and our neighbor William Law. What would his case be when he met Uncle Joseph at the bar of God? And what of Joseph Jackson? He had done his foul deed. The blood of the martyrs would stay on his hands for all the ages of eternity. I could feel only pity for him. Once I had told him he would be undone if he pursued his course. He had undone himself by killing the prophets of God.

Brother Phelps continued, "The prophet and patriarch have gone to paradise to bear testimony of the wickedness of the world, and help hasten the deliverance of the Saints."

"To the real mourners, and all Saints are such, let me say, mourn not; these sons of God are safe. Dry up your tears; confess the hand of the Lord in all things, and comfort each other with the sweet hope that their lives were precious in the sight of all heaven. Urge not the gentiles to punish their criminals; neither seek revenge, but soothe one another with the promise that the harvest of the earth is nigh and that vengeance belongs to the Lord and he will repay. Our Savior said, pray for thine enemies. So when they rage, pray; when they revel, fast; when they kill, watch; when nation wars with nation, hark; when judgments sweep, die; and when Jehovah speaks, do; that in the hour of woe every Saint may live by faith and be ready to enter into that joy which eye hath not seen, ear hath not heard, nor a heart of flesh thought of—the endless peace of God."

Chapter Thirty-three

Walking past the guards, who hushed at my presence, I sought the river for solace. How could it still flow? How could the sun shine and the birds fly when I was so heart-weary? Mobs raged against us. We were stricken with dread that at any moment we would be tossed upon the waves of extermination. Yet the river flowed. How could this be?

Brother Richards had pledged his life that we as a people would not retaliate the murders of my father and uncle. We had stayed at home peaceably. Was this not testimony enough of our intentions to keep the peace? We trusted in the law. Was it now to turn upon *us*, as it had upon our leaders?

I knelt down on a rock and placed my hands in the water. "Oh river," I pleaded, "would that you could tell your history! You who washed away the filth from our land, why are you subsiding at this time?" I asked with clenched fists. I looked up. "Oh sun, why, when all nature stopped for the death of the martyrs of truth, do you now shine so brightly for our danger?"

"Maybe there is no danger," came my answer from the Holy Ghost.

And that proved true. The mobs, spent and tired of their thirst for blood and finding themselves not avenged by the Legion, disbanded. They went back to their neglected and flooded fields and families. Life went on. The river knew. The sun knew. All nature knew. And God knew.

Hats were sold and strawberries were harvested on the land. Bricks were laid and nails were hammered. Cows were milked. And the creditors wanted their money. Who would pay them, the Church or the Smiths? It was time to settle the legal matters.

"I don't believe that Lorin and Lovina's marriage was entered on the records of the city," said Grandma Smith. She wanted everything settled properly.

So Lorin and I went to Aaron Johnson, the justice of the peace, to be married a second time. It was duly and properly entered on the records of the city. Now we were legal and could receive our share.

I had to sign the record book of the city. There was a place for Father to sign, too. But he could not! My pen stilled. My loss was too great. Blinded by tears, I stumbled out of the office.

Lorin followed close behind. When he caught up to me, he took me by the shoulders and faced me towards the temple.

"Lovina," he said, "I've been doing a powerful amount of pondering about what has befallen us. I thought whilst I was out on the prairies and while I was comforting Sister Emma. I know you're still grieving. We all are. But I want you to look at the temple on the hill. It stands there like a light set on a bushel. It is the first thing you see when you come up the river. It's the most imposing and important building in Nauvoo. Brother Joseph and Brother Hyrum gave us that fine building. And that was why we built this city—so we could gather to build the temple and make covenants with the Lord. When we make those covenants we will have the power to triumph over all our enemies, more power than ten Nauvoo Legions could give us. We will have the power to prevail.

"Today we were married by law, but it doesn't mean anything. What your father died for was for you to have the privilege of going to that temple when it's finished, and making our marriage eternal. If he hadn't died, the state mobs might have come and destroyed it. While he lived, he married us for time, but by dying he gave us the chance to finish that temple so you and I can be married, not just for time, but forever. He laid down his life for that building. He loved it. He loved us.

"And we're going to build it—you and I and the others. We're going to work and sweat and make your father and your uncle proud of us. We owe it to them."

I stared up at the hill. I saw the walls that were only one story high and needed finishing. The roof needed adding on that fall, then the glass bought with the Penny Fund could be put into place. Could we do it? As I looked at that glistening building of eternal hope that had gathered the faithful to it, my soul cried out, "Yes!" We would finish it for Father! Then we would build upon his work—a work that would go on and on, never to stop. Lorin and I would be married for eternity and continue to progress, worlds without end, with father, mother, sisters, brothers, and children. We would be sealed together, never to part again. What comfort that brought!

And there we'll join the heav'nly choir,
and sing His praise above;
While endless ages roll around,
Perfected by his love.

Epilogue

Lorin and Lovina Walker were sealed in the Nauvoo Temple on 28 January 1846. They remained with Emma Smith until she married Major Bidamon in December of 1847, then moved to the Ramus Stake in Illinois. With the help of Lorin's brother William, they emigrated west in 1856 and settled in Farmington, Utah, in 1860. Lovina bore Lorin thirteen children before she died in 1876.

Lorin and his second wife, Mary Middlemus, settled in Rockland, Idaho, where he died in 1907. The last years of his life were spent serving in the temple with his brothers and sisters.

Emma Smith Bidamon remained in Nauvoo in the Mansion House after Joseph was martyred. Grandma Lucy Mack Smith lived with her until she died in 1856, the year Lovina and Lorin went west. Uncle Samuel Smith died a month after the martyrdom from wounds suffered in his attempt to rescue his brothers.

Lorin's father, John Walker, returned from his mission, remarried, and took his family west with the Saints. His sister Lucy married Heber C. Kimball and bore him nine children.

Lovina's stepmother, Mary Fielding Smith, went west with the main body of the Saints, together with her sister Mercy and brother Joseph Fielding.

Eliza Partridge was a courageous woman who had a very difficult life. She married Amasa Lyman, who later apostacized, and she was left alone to raise her family. Her sister Emily became the wife of Brigham Young.

In August of 1844, Joseph Jackson published "A Narrative of the Adventures and Experiences of Joseph H. Jackson in

Nauvoo, Disclosing the Depths of Mormon Villany," from Warsaw, Illinois. He was legally charged with murder in September of 1944, along with Colonel Levi Williams and Thomas Sharpe, editor of the *Warsaw Signal*. When law enforcement officers apprehended these men, Jackson was so sick that he could not be taken. He was never tried and disappeared from the scene. Even the harshest critics of Joseph Smith view Jackson as a prevaricating opportunist.

Governor Ford died a pauper less than ten years after the martyrdom.

About the Author

Becky Paget was born and raised in Allentown, Pennsylvania. As a young woman, she had two great loves—art and reading. She graduated from Brigham Young University with a Bachelor of Fine Arts degree in drawing and painting, but her continuing interest in literature compelled her to write. Her first novel, *Romancing the Nephites,* was published by Covenant in 1993, and she says that writing *The Belle of Nauvoo* has been one of the most marvelous spiritual experiences of her life.

Converted to the Church at age 15, Becky teaches early-morning seminary. She also serves as a docent for Laumeier Sculpture Park, does freelance art from her home, and performs as a cast member in the annual "City of Joseph" outdoor musical production. She and her husband, Jon, live with their four children in St. Louis, Missouri.